By Neil Gaiman and published by Headline

The View From The Cheap Seats
Trigger Warning
The Ocean at the End of the Lane
Fragile Things
Anansi Boys
American Gods
Stardust
Smoke and Mirrors
Neverwhere

How the Marquis Got His Coat Back
(a Neverwhere *short story)*

Illustrated editions

American Gods
Anansi Boys
The Monarch of the Glen
Black Dog
(illustrated by Daniel Egnéus)

Neverwhere
(illustrated by Chris Riddell)

The Truth is a Cave in the Black Mountains
(illustrated by Eddie Campbell)

How to Talk to Girls at Parties
(adaptation and artwork by Fábio Moon and Gabriel Bá)

Troll Bridge
(Adaptation and artwork by Colleen Doran)

MirrorMask: The Illustrated Film Script
(with Dave McKean)

NEIL GAIMAN
THE MONARCH OF THE GLEN

ILLUSTRATED BY
DANIEL EGNÉUS

Copyright © 2004 Neil Gaiman

The right of Neil Gaiman to be identified as the Author of
the Work has been asserted by him in accordance with
the Copyright, Designs and Patents Act 1988.

Illustrations copyright © 2016 Daniel Egnéus

The right of Daniel Egnéus to be identified as the Illustrator of
the Work has been asserted by him in accordance with the
Copyright, Designs and Patents Act 1988.

'The Lady of the House of Love' taken from
The Bloody Chamber and Other Stories © Angela Carter 1979
First published in Great Britain by Victor Gollancz Ltd, 1979

First published in *Legends II*

Then published in *Fragile Things* in Great Britain in 2006 by
HEADLINE REVIEW
An imprint of HEADLINE BOOK PUBLISHING

First published in *Fragile Things* in paperback in Great Britain in 2007 by
HEADLINE REVIEW

This edition published in 2016 by
HEADLINE PUBLISHING GROUP

1

Apart from any use permitted under UK copyright law, this publication may only
be reproduced, stored, or transmitted, in any form, or by any means, with prior permission
in writing of the publishers or, in the case of reprographic production, in accordance with
the terms of licences issued by the Copyright Licensing Agency.

All characters in this publication are fictitious and any resemblance
to real persons, living or dead, is purely coincidental.

ISBN 978 1 4722 3543 5

Typeset in Zapf Elliptical and Priori Serif by Patrick Insole

Printed and bound in Great Britain by Clays Ltd, St Ives plc

Headline's policy is to use papers that are natural, renewable and recyclable products and
made from wood grown in sustainable forests. The logging and manufacturing processes
are expected to conform to the environmental regulations of the country of origin.

HEADLINE PUBLISHING GROUP
An Hachette UK Company
Carmelite House
50 Victoria Embankment
London, EC4Y 0DZ

www.headline.co.uk
www.hachette.co.uk

To Matthew and Claudia,
for hospitality
N. G.

For Eva and Sussi
D. E.

'She herself is a haunted house. She does not possess herself; her ancestors sometimes come and peer out of the windows of her eyes and that is very frightening.'
    Angela Carter, 'The Lady of the House of Love'

I

'If you ask me,' said the little man to Shadow, 'you're something of a monster. Am I right?'

They were the only two people, apart from the barmaid, in the bar of a hotel in a town on the north coast of Scotland. Shadow had been sitting there on his own, drinking a lager, when the man came over and sat at his table. It was late summer, and it seemed to Shadow that everything was cold, and small, and damp. He had a small book of Pleasant Local Walks in front of him, and was studying the walk he planned to do tomorrow, along the coast, towards Cape Wrath.

He closed the book.

'I'm American,' said Shadow. 'If that's what you mean.'

The little man cocked his head to one side, and he winked, theatrically. He had steel-grey hair, and a grey face, and a grey coat, and he looked like a small-town lawyer. 'Well, perhaps that is what I mean, at that,' he said.

Shadow had had problems understanding Scottish accents in his short time in the country, all rich burrs and strange words and trills, but he had no trouble understanding this man. Everything the little man said was small and crisp, each word so perfectly enunciated that it made Shadow feel like he himself was talking with a mouthful of oatmeal.

The little man sipped his drink and said, 'So you're American. Oversexed, overpaid and over here. Eh? D'you work on the rigs?'

'Sorry?'

'An oilman? Out on the big metal platforms. We get oil people up here, from time to time.'

'No. I'm not from the rigs.'

The little man took out a pipe from his pocket, and a small penknife, and began to remove the dottle from the bowl. Then he tapped it out into the ashtray. 'They have oil in Texas, you know,' he said, after a while, as if he were confiding a great secret. 'That's in America.'

'Yes,' said Shadow. He thought about saying something about Texans believing that Texas was actually in Texas, but he suspected that he'd have to start explaining what he meant, so he said nothing.

Shadow had been away from America for the better part of two years. He had been away when the towers fell. He told himself sometimes that he did not care if he ever went back, and sometimes he almost came close to believing himself. He had reached the Scottish mainland two days ago, landed in Thurso on the ferry from the Orkneys, and had travelled to the town he was staying in by bus.

The little man was talking. 'So there's a Texas oilman, down in Aberdeen, he's talking to an old fellow he meets in a pub, much like you and me meeting, actually, and they get talking, and the Texan, he says, "Back in Texas I get up in the morning, I get into my car" – I won't try to do the accent, if you don't mind – "I'll turn the key in the ignition, and put my foot down on the accelerator", what you call the, the—'

'Gas pedal,' said Shadow, helpfully.

'Right. "Put my foot down on the gas pedal at breakfast, and by lunchtime I still won't have reached the edge of my property." And the canny old Scot, he just nods and says, "Aye, well, I used to have a car like that myself." ' The little man laughed raucously, to show that the joke was done. Shadow smiled, and nodded, to show that he knew it was a joke.

'What are you drinking? Lager? Same again over here, Jennie love. Mine's a Lagavulin.' The little man tamped tobacco from a pouch into his pipe. 'Did you know that Scotland's bigger than America?'

There had been no one in the hotel bar when Shadow came downstairs that evening, just the thin barmaid, reading a newspaper and smoking her cigarette. He'd come down to sit by the open fire, as his bedroom was cold, and the metal radiators on the bedroom wall were colder than the room. He hadn't expected company.

'No,' said Shadow, always willing to play straight man. 'I didn't. How'd you reckon that?'

'It's all fractal,' said the little man. 'The smaller you look, the more things unpack. It could take you as long to drive across America as it would to drive across Scotland, if you did it the right way. It's like, you look on a map, and the coastlines are solid lines. But when you walk them, they're all over the place. I saw a whole programme on it on the telly the other night. Great stuff.'

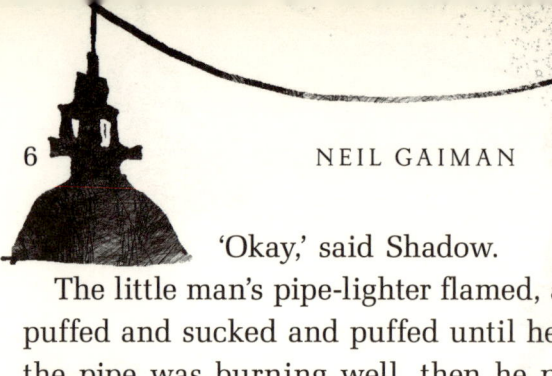

'Okay,' said Shadow.

The little man's pipe-lighter flamed, and he sucked and puffed and sucked and puffed until he was satisfied that the pipe was burning well, then he put the lighter, the pouch and the penknife back into his coat pocket.

'Anyway, anyway,' said the little man. 'I believe you're planning on staying here through the weekend.'

'Yes,' said Shadow. 'Do you . . . are you with the hotel?'

'No, no. Truth to tell, I was standing in the hall when you arrived. I heard you talking to Gordon on the reception desk.'

Shadow nodded. He had thought that he had been alone in the reception hall when he had registered, but it was possible that the little man had passed through. But still . . . there was a wrongness to this conversation. There was a wrongness to everything.

Jennie the barmaid put their drinks on to the bar. 'Five pounds twenty,' she said. She picked up her newspaper, and started to read once more. The little man went to the bar, paid, and brought back the drinks.

'So how long are you in Scotland?' asked the little man.

Shadow shrugged. 'I wanted to see what it was like. Take some walks. See the sights. Maybe a week. Maybe a month.'

Jennie put down her newspaper. 'It's the arse-end of nowhere up here,' she said, cheerfully. 'You should go somewhere interesting.'

'That's where you're wrong,' said the little man. 'It's only the arse-end of nowhere if you look at it wrong. See that map, laddie?' He pointed to a fly-specked map of northern Scotland on the opposite wall of the bar. 'You know what's wrong with it?'

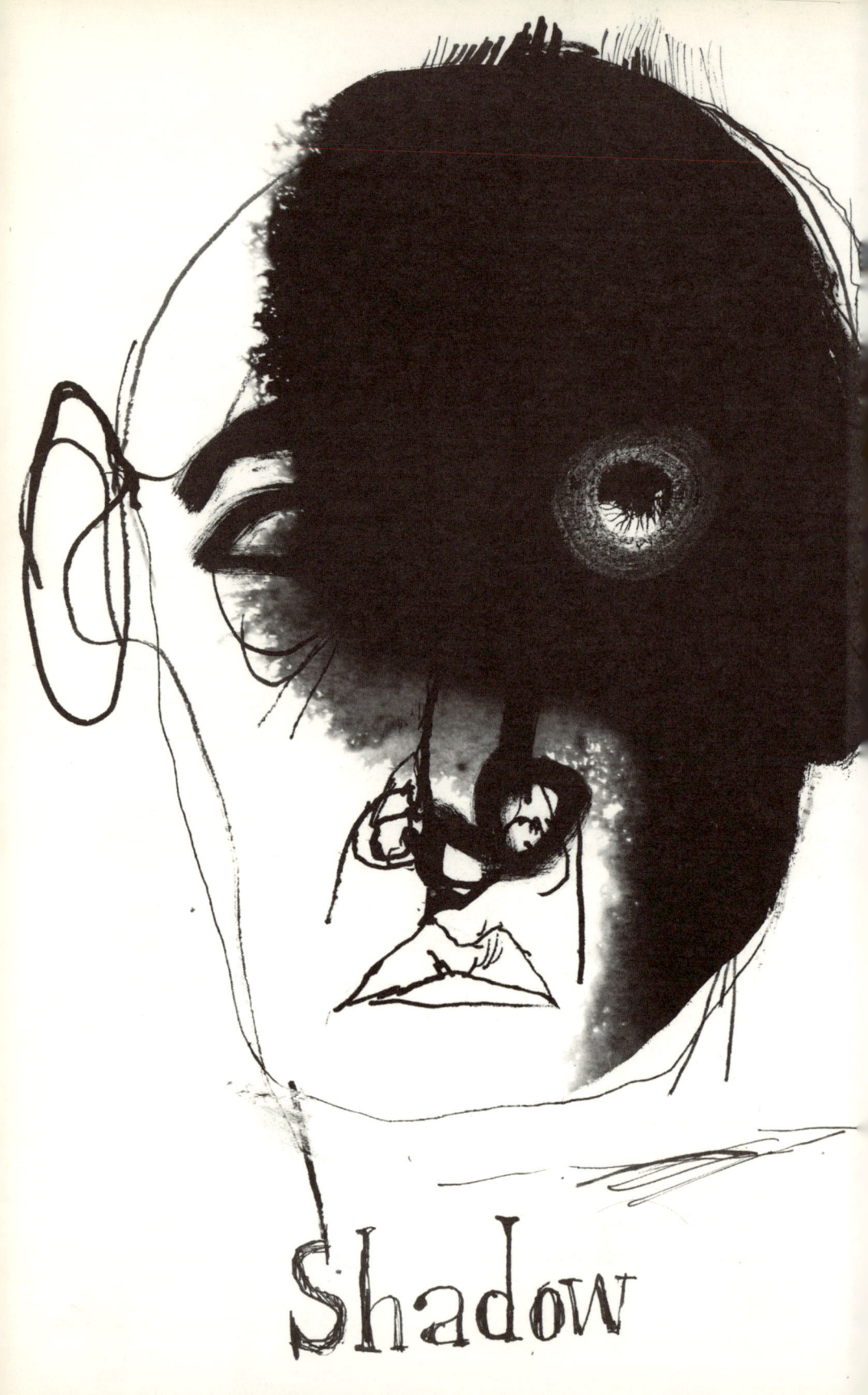

'No.'

'It's upside-down!' the man said, triumphantly. 'North's at the top. It's saying to the world that this is where things stop. Go no further. The world ends here. But, you see, that's not how it was. This wasn't the north of Scotland. This was the southernmost tip of the Viking world. You know what the second most northern county in Scotland is called?'

Shadow glanced at the map, but it was too far away to read. He shook his head.

'Sutherland!' said the little man. He showed his teeth. 'The South Land. Not to anyone else in the world it wasn't, but it was to the Vikings.'

Jennie the barmaid walked over to them. 'I won't be gone long,' she said. 'Call the front desk if you need anything before I get back.' She put a log on the fire, then she went out into the hall.

'Are you a historian?' Shadow asked.

'Good one,' said the little man. 'You may be a monster, but you're funny. I'll give you that.'

'I'm not a monster,' said Shadow.

'Aye, that's what monsters always say,' said the little man. 'I was a specialist once. In St Andrews. Now I'm in general practice. Well, I was. I'm semi-retired. Go into the surgery a couple of days a week, just to keep my hand in.'

'Why do you say I'm a monster?' asked Shadow.

'Because,' said the little man, lifting his whisky glass with the air of one making an irrefutable point, 'I am something of a monster myself. Like calls to like. We are all monsters, are we not? Glorious monsters, shambling through the swamps of unreason . . .' He sipped his whisky, then said, 'Tell me, a big man like you, have you ever been a bouncer? "Sorry mate, I'm afraid you can't come in here tonight, private function going on, sling your hook and get on out of it", all that?'

'No,' said Shadow.

'But you must have done something like that?'

'Yes,' said Shadow, who had been a bodyguard once, to an old god; but that was in another country.

'You, uh, you'll pardon me for asking, don't take this the wrong way, but do you need money?'

'Everyone needs money. But I'm okay.' This was not entirely true; but it was a truth that, when Shadow needed money, the world seemed to go out of its way to provide it.

'Would you like to make a wee bit of spending money? Being a bouncer? It's a piece of piss. Money for old rope.'

'At a disco?'

'Not exactly. A private party. They rent a big old house near here, come in from all over at the end of the summer. So last year, everybody's having a grand old time, champagne out of doors, all that, and there was some trouble. A bad lot. Out to ruin everybody's weekend.'

'These were locals?'

'I don't think so.'

'Was it political?' asked Shadow. He did not want to be drawn into local politics.

'Not a bit of it. Yobs and hairies and idiots. Anyway. They probably won't come back this year. Probably off in the wilds of nowhere demonstrating against international capitalism. But just to be on the safe side, the folk up at the house've asked me to look out for someone who could do a spot of intimidating. You're a big lad, and that's what they want.'

'How much?' asked Shadow.

'Can you handle yourself in a fight, if it came down to it?' asked the man.

Shadow didn't say anything. The little man looked Shadow up and down, and then he grinned again, showing tobacco-stained teeth. 'Fifteen hundred pounds, for a long weekend's work. That's good money. And it's cash. Nothing you'd ever need to report to the taxman.'

'This weekend coming?' said Shadow.

'Starting Friday morning. It's a big old house. Part of it used to be a castle. West of Cape Wrath.'

'I don't know,' said Shadow.

'If you do it,' said the little grey man, 'you'll get a fantastic weekend in a historical house, and I can guarantee you'll get to meet all kinds of interesting people. Perfect holiday job. I just wish I was younger. And, uh, a great deal taller, actually.'

Shadow said, 'Okay,' and, as soon as he said it, wondered if he would regret it.

'Good man. I'll get you more details as and when.' The little grey man stood up, and gave Shadow's shoulder a gentle pat as he walked past. Then he went out, leaving Shadow in the bar on his own.

II

Shadow had been on the road for about eighteen months. He had backpacked across Europe and down into northern Africa. He had picked olives, and fished for sardines, and driven a truck, and sold wine from the side of a road. Finally, several months ago, he had hitchhiked his way back to Norway, to Oslo, where he had been born thirty-five years before.

He was not sure what he had been looking for. He only knew that he had not found it, although there were moments, in the high ground, in the crags and waterfalls, when he was certain that whatever he needed was just around the corner: behind a jut of granite, or in the nearest pinewood.

Still, it was a deeply unsatisfactory visit, and when, in Bergen, he was asked if he would be half of the crew of a motor-yacht, on its way to meet its owner in Cannes, he said yes.

They had sailed from Bergen to the Shetlands, and then to the Orkneys, where they spent the night in a bed and

breakfast in Stromness. Next morning, leaving the harbour, the engines had failed, ultimately and irrevocably, and the boat had been towed back to port.

Bjorn, who was the captain and the other half of the crew, stayed with the boat, to talk to the insurers and field the angry calls from the boat's owner. Shadow saw no reason to stay: he took the ferry to Thurso, on the north coast of Scotland.

He was restless. At night he dreamed of freeways, of entering the neon edges of a city where the people spoke English. Sometimes it was in the Midwest, sometimes it was in Florida, sometimes on the East Coast, sometimes on the West.

When he got off the ferry he bought a book of scenic walks, and picked up a bus timetable, and he set off into the world.

Jennie the barmaid came back, and started to wipe all the surfaces with a cloth. Her hair was so blonde it was almost white, and it was tied up at the back in a bun.

'So what is it people do around here for fun?' asked Shadow.

'They drink. They wait to die,' she said. 'Or they go south. That pretty much exhausts your options.'

'You sure?'

'Well, think about it. There's nothing up here but sheep and hills. We feed off the tourists, of course, but there's never really enough of you. Sad, isn't it?'

Shadow shrugged.

'Are you from New York?' she asked.

'Chicago, originally. But I came here from Norway.'

'You speak Norwegian?'

'A little.'

'There's somebody you should meet,' she said, suddenly. Then she looked at her watch. 'Somebody who came here from Norway, a long time ago. Come on.'

She put her cleaning cloth down, turned off the barlights, and walked over to the door. 'Come on,' she said, again.

'Can you do that?' asked Shadow.

'I can do whatever I want,' she said. 'It's a free country, isn't it?'

'I guess.'

She locked the bar with a brass key. They walked into the reception hall. 'Wait here,' she said. She went through a door marked PRIVATE, and reappeared several minutes later, wearing a long brown coat. 'Okay. Follow me.'

They walked out into the street. 'So, is this a village or a small town?' asked Shadow.

'It's a fucking graveyard,' she said. 'Up this way. Come on.'

They walked up a narrow road. The moon was huge and a yellowish brown. Shadow could hear the sea, although he could not yet see it. 'You're Jennie?' he said.

'That's right. And you?'

'Shadow.'

'Is that your real name?'

'It's what they call me.'

'Come on, then, Shadow,' she said.

At the top of the hill, they stopped. They were on the edge of the village, and there was a grey stone cottage. Jennie opened the gate, and led Shadow up a path to the front door. He brushed a small bush at the side of the path, and the air filled with the scent of sweet lavender. There were no lights on in the cottage.

'Whose house is this?' asked Shadow. 'It looks empty.'

'Don't worry,' said Jennie. 'She'll be home in a second.'

She pushed open the unlocked front door, and they went inside. She turned on the light switch by the door. Most of the inside of the cottage was taken up by a kitchen-sitting room. There was a tiny staircase leading up to what Shadow presumed was an attic bedroom. A CD player sat on the pine counter.

'This is your house,' said Shadow.

'Home sweet home,' she agreed. 'You want coffee? Or something to drink?'

'Neither,' said Shadow. He wondered what Jennie wanted. She had barely looked at him, hadn't even smiled at him.

'Did I hear right? Was Doctor Gaskell asking you to help look after a party on the weekend?'

'I guess.'

'So what are you doing tomorrow and Friday?'

'Walking,' said Shadow. 'I've got a book. There are some beautiful walks.'

NEIL GAIMAN

'Some of them are beautiful. Some of them are treacherous,' she told him. 'You can still find winter snow here, in the shadows, in the summer. Things last a long time, in the shadows.'

'I'll be careful,' he told her.

'That was what the Vikings said,' she said, and she smiled. She took off her coat and dropped it on the bright purple sofa. 'Maybe I'll see you out there. I like to go for walks.' She pulled at the bun at the back of her head, and her pale hair fell free. It was longer than Shadow had thought it would be.

'Do you live here alone?'

She took a cigarette from a packet on the counter, lit it with a match. 'What's it to you?' she asked. 'You won't be staying the night, will you?'

Shadow shook his head.

'The hotel's at the bottom of the hill,' she told him. 'You can't miss it. Thanks for walking me home.'

Shadow said good-night, and walked back, through the lavender night, out to the lane. He stood there for a little while, staring at the moon on the sea, puzzled. Then he walked down the hill until he got to the hotel. She was right: you couldn't miss it. He walked up the stairs, unlocked his room with a key attached to a short stick, and went inside. The room was colder than the corridor.

He took off his shoes, and stretched out on the bed in the dark.

III

The ship was made of the fingernails of dead men, and it lurched through the mist, bucking and rolling hugely and unsteadily on the choppy sea.

There were shadowy shapes on the deck, men as big as hills or houses, and as Shadow got closer he could see their faces: proud men and tall, each one of them. They seemed to ignore the ship's motion, each man waiting on the deck as if frozen in place.

One of them stepped forward, and he grasped Shadow's hand with his own huge hand. Shadow stepped on to the grey deck.

'Well come to this accursed place,' said the man holding Shadow's hand, in a deep, gravel voice.

'Hail!' called the men on the deck. 'Hail sun-bringer! Hail Baldur!'

The name on Shadow's birth certificate was Balder Moon, but he shook his head. 'I am not him,' he told them. 'I am not the one you are waiting for.'

'We are dying here,' said the gravel-voiced man, not letting go of Shadow's hand.

It was cold in the misty place between the worlds of waking and the grave. Salt spray crashed on the bows of the grey ship, and Shadow was drenched to the skin.

'Bring us back,' said the man holding his hand. 'Bring us back or let us go.'

Shadow said, 'I don't know how.'

At that, the men on the deck began to wail and howl. Some of them crashed the hafts of their spears against the deck, others struck the flats of their short swords against the brass bowls at the centre of their leather shields, setting up a rhythmic din accompanied by cries that moved from sorrow to a full-throated berserker ululation . . .

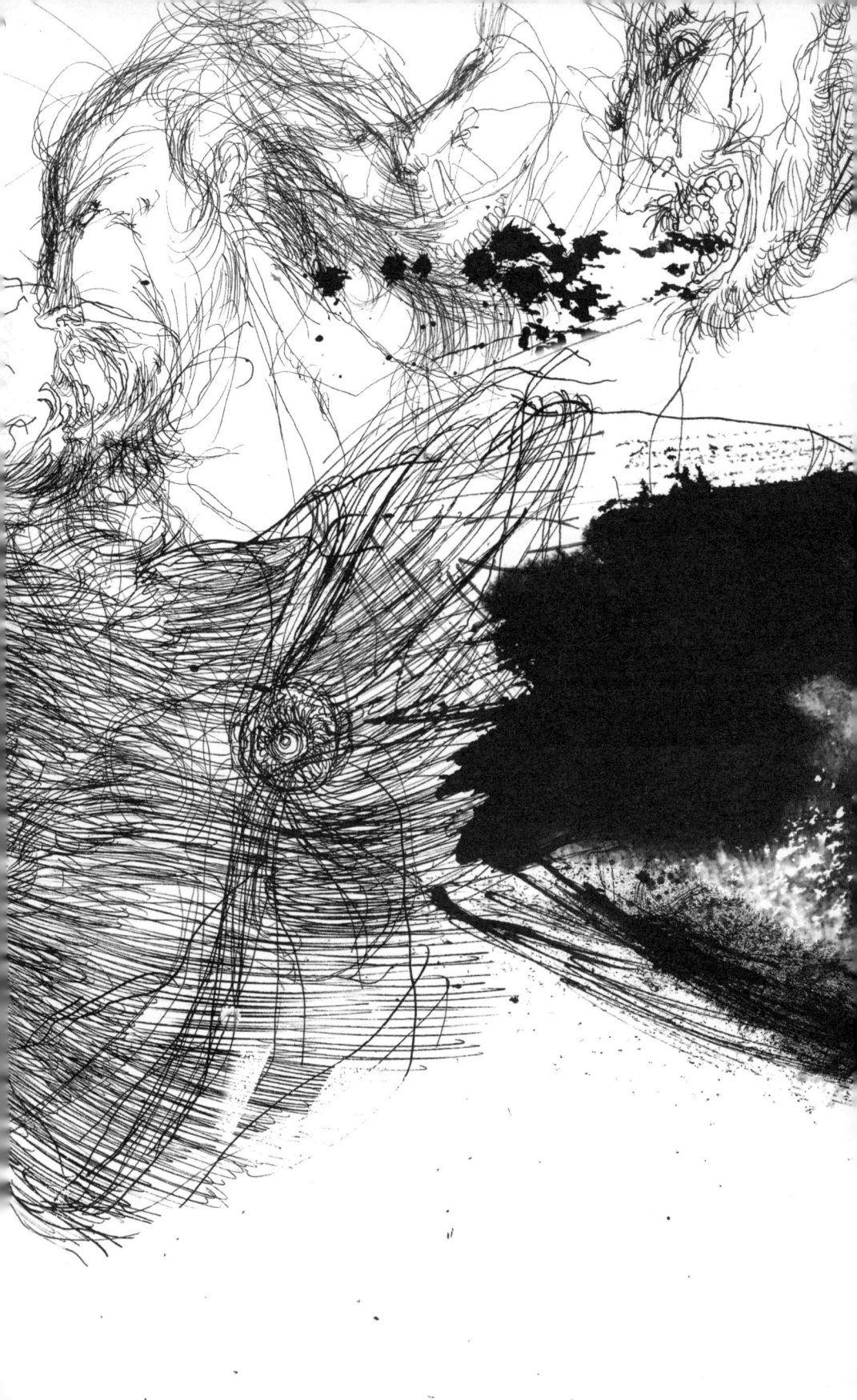

NEIL GAIMAN

A seagull was screaming in the early morning air. The bedroom window had blown open in the night, and was bang ing in the wind. Shadow was lying on the top of his bed in his narrow hotel room. His skin was damp, perhaps with sweat.

Another cold day at the end of the summer had begun.

The hotel packed him a Tupperware box containing several chicken sandwiches, a hard-boiled egg, a small packet of cheese-and-onion crisps, and an apple. Gordon on the reception desk, who handed him the box, asked when he'd be back, explaining that if he was more than a couple of hours late they'd call out the rescue services, and asking for the number of Shadow's mobile phone.

Shadow did not have a mobile phone.

He set off on the walk, heading towards the coast. It was beautiful, a desolate beauty that chimed and echoed with the empty places inside Shadow. He had imagined Scotland as being a soft place, all gentle heathery hills, but here on the north coast everything seemed sharp and jutting, even the grey clouds that scudded across the pale blue sky. It was as if the bones of the world showed through. He followed the route in his book, across scrubby meadows and past splashing burns, up rocky hills and down.

Sometimes he imagined that he was standing still and the world was moving underneath him, that he was simply pushing it past with his legs.

The route was more tiring than he had expected. He had planned to eat at one o'clock, but by midday his legs were tired and he wanted a break. He followed his path to the side of a hill, where a boulder provided a convenient windbreak, and he crouched to eat his lunch. In the distance, ahead of him, he could see the Atlantic.

He had thought himself alone.

She said, 'Will you give me your apple?'

It was Jennie, the barmaid from the hotel. Her too-fair hair gusted about her head.

'Hello, Jennie,' said Shadow. He passed her his apple.

She pulled a clasp-knife from the pocket of her brown coat, and sat beside him. 'Thanks,' she said.

'So,' said Shadow, 'from your accent, you must have come from Norway when you were a kid. I mean, you sound like a local to me.'

'Did I say that I came from Norway?'

'Well, didn't you?'

She speared an apple slice, and ate it, fastidiously, from the tip of the knife blade, only touching it with her teeth. She glanced at him. 'It was a long time ago.'

'Family?'

She moved her shoulders in a shrug, as if any answer she could give him was beneath her.

'So you like it here?'

She looked at him and shook her head. 'I feel like a *hulder*.'

He'd heard the word before, in Norway. 'Aren't they a kind of troll?'

'No. They are mountain creatures, like the trolls, but they come from the woods, and they are very beautiful. Like me.' She grinned as she said it, as if she knew that she was too pallid, too sulky and too thin ever to be beautiful. 'They fall in love with farmers.'

'Why?'

'Damned if I know,' she said. 'But they do. Sometimes the farmer realises that he is talking to a *hulder* woman, because she has a cow's tail hanging down behind, or worse,

sometimes from behind there is nothing there, she is just hollow and empty, like a shell. Then the farmer says a prayer, or runs away, flees back to his mother or his farm.

'But sometimes the farmers do not run. Sometimes they throw a knife over her shoulder, or just smile, and they marry the *huldra* woman. Then her tail falls off. But she is still stronger than any human woman could ever be. And she still pines for her home in the forests and the mountains. She will never be truly happy. She will never be human.'

'What happens to her then?' asked Shadow. 'Does she age and die with her farmer?'

She had sliced the apple down to the core. Now, with a flick of the wrist, she sent the apple core arcing off the side of the hill. 'When her man dies . . . I think she goes back to the hills and the woods.' She stared out at the hillside. 'There's a story about one of them who was married to a

farmer who didn't treat her well. He shouted at her, wouldn't help around the farm, he came home from the village drunk and angry. Sometimes he beat her.

'Now, one day she's in the farmhouse, making up the morning's fire, and he comes in and starts shouting at her, for his food is not ready, and he is angry, nothing she does is right, he doesn't know why he married her, and she listens to him for a while, and then, saying nothing, she reaches down to the fireplace, and she picks up the poker. A heavy black iron jobbie. She takes that poker and, without an effort, she bends it into a perfect circle, just like her wedding ring. She doesn't grunt or sweat, she just bends it, like you'd bend a reed. And her farmer sees this and he goes white as a sheet, and doesn't

say anything else about his breakfast. He's seen what she did to the poker and he knows that at any time in the last five years she could have done the same to him. And until he died, he never laid another finger on her, never said one harsh word. Now, you tell me something, Mister everybodycalls-you-Shadow, if she could do that, why did she let him beat her in the first place? Why would she want to be with someone like that? You tell me.'

'Maybe,' said Shadow, 'maybe she was lonely.'

She wiped the blade of the knife on her jeans.

'Dr Gaskell kept saying you were a monster,' she said. 'Is it true?'

'I don't think so,' said Shadow.

'Pity,' she said. 'You know where you are with monsters, don't you?'

'You do?'

'Absolutely. At the end of the day, you're going to be dinner. Talking about which, I'll show you something.' She stood up, and led him to the top of the hill. 'See. Over there? On the far side of that hill, where it drops into the glen, you can just see the house you'll be working at this weekend. Do you see it, over there?'

'No.'

'Look. I'll point. Follow the line of my finger.' She stood close to him, held out her hand and pointed to the side of a distant ridge. He could see the overhead sun glinting off something he supposed was a lake – or a loch, he corrected himself, he was in Scotland after all – and above that a grey outcropping on the side of a hill. He had taken it for rocks, but it was too regular to be anything but a building.

'That's the castle?'

'I'd not call it that. Just a big house in the glen.'

'Have you been to one of the parties there?'

'They don't invite locals,' she said. 'And they wouldn't ask me. You shouldn't do it, anyway. You should say no.'

'They're paying good money,' he told her.

She touched him then, for the first time, placed her pale fingers on the back of his dark hand. 'And what good is money to a monster?' she asked, and smiled, and Shadow was damned if he didn't think that maybe she *was* beautiful, at that.

And then she put down her hand and backed away. 'Well?' she said. 'Shouldn't you be off on your walk? You've not got much longer before you'll have to start heading back again. The light goes fast when it goes, this time of year.'

And she stood and watched him as he hefted his rucksack, and began to walk down the hill. He turned around when he reached the bottom and looked up. She was still looking at him. He waved, and she waved back.

The next time he looked back she was gone.

He took the little ferry across the kyle to the cape, and walked up to the lighthouse. There was a minibus from the lighthouse back to the ferry, and he took it.

He got back to the hotel at eight that night, exhausted

but feeling satisfied. It had rained once, in the late afternoon, but he had taken shelter in a tumbledown bothy, and read a five-year-old newspaper while the rain drummed against the roof. It had ended after half an hour, but Shadow had been glad that he had good boots, for the earth had turned to mud.

He was starving. He went into the hotel restaurant. It was empty. Shadow said, 'Hello?'

An elderly woman came to the door between the restaurant and the kitchen and said, 'Aye?'

'Are you still serving dinner?'

'Aye.' She looked at him disapprovingly, from his muddy boots to his tousled hair. 'Are you a guest?'

'Yes. I'm in room eleven.'

'Well . . . you'll probably want to change before dinner,' she said. 'It's kinder to the other diners.'

'So you *are* serving.'

'Aye.'

He went up to his room, dropped his rucksack on the bed, and took off his boots. He put on his sneakers, ran a comb through his hair, and went back downstairs.

The dining room was no longer empty. Two people were sitting at a table in the corner, two people who seemed different in every way that people could be different: a small woman who looked to be in her late fifties, hunched and birdlike at the table, and a young man, big and awkward and perfectly bald. Shadow decided that they were mother and son.

He sat down at a table in the centre of the room.

The elderly waitress came in with a tray. She gave both of the other diners a bowl of soup. The man began to blow on his soup, to cool it; his mother tapped him, hard, on the back of his hand, with her spoon. 'Stop that,' she said. She began to spoon the soup into her mouth, slurping it noisily.

The bald man looked around the room sadly. He caught Shadow's eye, and Shadow nodded at him. The man sighed, and returned to his steaming soup.

Shadow scanned the menu without enthusiasm. He was ready to order, but the waitress had vanished again.

A flash of grey; Dr Gaskell peered in at the door of the restaurant. He walked into the room, came over to Shadow's table. 'Do you mind if I join you?'

'Not at all. Please. Sit down.'

He sat down, opposite Shadow. 'Have a good day?'

'Very good. I walked.'

'Best way to work up an appetite. So. First thing tomorrow they're sending a car out here to pick you up. Bring your things. They'll take you out to the house. Show you the ropes.'

'And the money?' asked Shadow.

'They'll sort that out. Half at the beginning, half at the end. Anything else you want to know?'

The waitress stood at the edge of the room, watching them, making no move to approach. 'Yeah. What do I have to do to get some food around here?'

'What do you want? I recommend the lamb chops. The lamb's local.'

'Sounds good.'

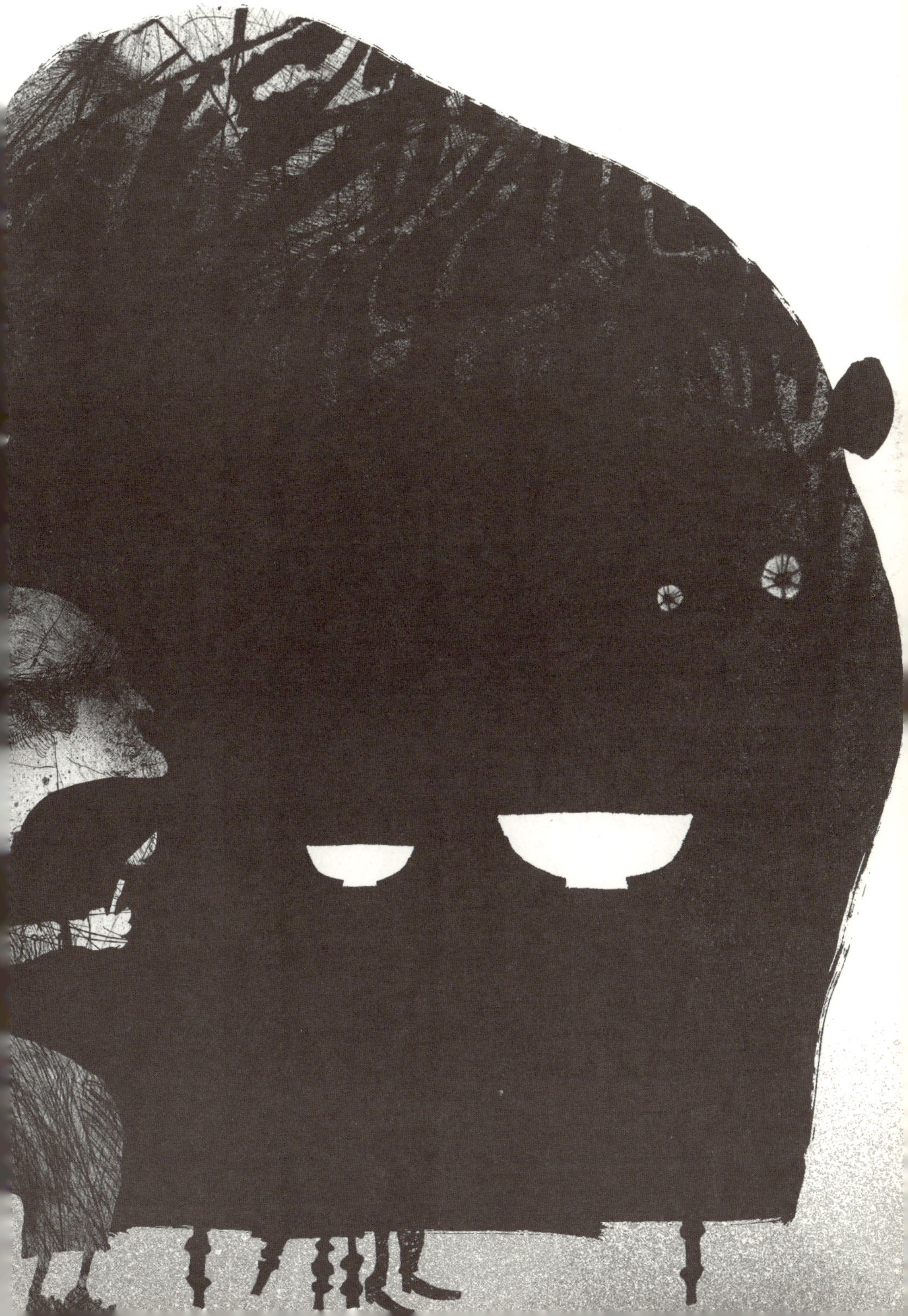

Dr Gaskell
steel hair

Gaskell said loudly, 'Excuse me, Maura. Sorry to trouble you, but could we both have the lamb chops?'

She pursed her lips, and went back to the kitchen.

'Thanks,' said Shadow.

'Don't mention it. Anything else I can help you with?'

'Yeah. These folk coming in for the party. Why don't they hire their own security? Why hire me?'

'They'll be doing that too, I have no doubt,' said Gaskell. 'Bringing in their own people. But it's good to have local talent.'

'Even if the local talent is a foreign tourist?'

'Just so.'

Maura brought two bowls of soup, put them down in front of Shadow and the doctor. 'They come with the meal,' she said. The soup was too hot, and it tasted faintly of reconstituted tomatoes and vinegar. Shadow was hungry enough that he'd finished most of the bowl off before he realised that he did not like it.

'You said I was a monster,' said Shadow, to the steel-grey man.

'I did?'

'You did.'

'Well, there's a lot of monsters in this part of the world.' He tipped his head towards the couple in the corner. The little woman had picked up her napkin, dipped it into her water-glass, and was dabbing vigorously with it at the spots of crimson soup on her son's mouth and chin. He looked embarrassed. 'It's remote. We don't get into the news unless a hiker or a climber gets lost, or starves to death. Most people forget we're here.'

The lamb chops arrived, on a plate with overboiled potatoes, underboiled carrots, and something brown and wet that Shadow thought might have started life as spinach. He started to cut at the chops with his knife. The doctor picked his up in his fingers, and began to chew.

'You've been inside,' said the doctor.

'Inside?'

'Prison. You've been in prison.' It wasn't a question.

'Yes.'

'So you know how to fight. You could hurt someone, if you had to.'

Shadow said, 'If you need someone to hurt people, I'm probably not the guy you're looking for.'

The little man grinned, with greasy grey lips. 'I'm sure you are. I was just asking. You can't give a man a hard time for asking. Anyway. *He's* a monster,' he said, gesturing across the room with a mostly chewed lamb chop. The bald man was eating some kind of white pudding with a spoon. 'So's his mother.'

'They don't look like monsters to me,' said Shadow.

'I'm teasing you, I'm afraid. Local sense of humour. They should warn you about mine when you enter the village. Warning, loony old doctor at work. Talking about monsters. Forgive an old man. You mustn't listen to a word I say.' A flash of tobacco-stained teeth. He wiped his hands and mouth on his napkin. 'Maura, we'll be needing the bill over here. The young man's dinner is on me.'

'Yes, Doctor Gaskell.'

'Remember,' said the doctor to Shadow. 'Eight fifteen tomorrow morning, be in the lobby. No later. They're busy people. If you aren't there, they'll just move on, and you'll have missed out on fifteen hundred pounds, for a weekend's work. A bonus, if they're happy.'

Shadow decided to have his after-dinner coffee in the bar. There was a log fire there, after all. He hoped it would take the chill from his bones.

Gordon from Reception was working behind the bar. 'Jennie's night off?' asked Shadow.

'What? No, she was just helping out. She'll do it if we're busy, sometimes.'

'Mind if I put another log on the fire?'

'Help yourself.'

If this is how the Scots treat their summers, thought Shadow, remembering something Oscar Wilde had once said, *they don't deserve to have any.*

The bald young man came in. He nodded a nervous greeting to Shadow. Shadow nodded back. The man had no hair that Shadow could see: no eyebrows, no eyelashes. It made him look babyish, and unformed. Shadow wondered if it was a disease, or if it was perhaps a side-effect of chemotherapy. He smelled of damp.

'I heard what he said,' stammered the bald man. 'He said I was a monster. He said my ma was a monster too. I've got good ears on me. I don't miss much.'

He did have good ears on him. They were a translucent pink, and they stuck out from the side of his head like the fins of some huge fish.

'You've got great ears,' said Shadow.

'You taking the mickey?' The bald man's tone was aggrieved. He looked like he was ready to fight. He was only a little shorter than Shadow, and Shadow was a big man.

'If that means what I think it does, not at all.'

The bald man nodded. 'That's good,' he said. He swallowed, and hesitated. Shadow wondered if he should say something conciliatory, but the bald man continued, 'It's not my fault. Making all that noise. I mean, people come up here to get away from the noise. And the people. Too many damned people up here anyway. Why don't you just go back to where you came from and stop making all that bluidy noise?'

The man's mother appeared in the doorway. She smiled nervously at Shadow, then walked hurriedly over to her son. She pulled at his sleeve. 'Now then,' she said. 'Don't you get yourself all worked up over nothing. Everything's all right.' She looked up at Shadow, bird-like, placatory. 'I'm sorry. I'm sure he didn't mean it.' She had a length of toilet paper sticking to the bottom of her shoe, and she hadn't noticed yet.

'Everything's all right,' said Shadow. 'It's good to meet people.'

She nodded. 'That's all right, then,' she said. Her son looked relieved. He's scared of her, thought Shadow.

'Come on, pet,' said the woman to her son. She pulled at his sleeve, and he followed her to the door.

Then he stopped, obstinately, and turned. 'You tell them,' said the bald young man, 'not to make so much noise.'

'I'll tell them,' said Shadow.

'It's just that I can hear everything.'

'Don't worry about it,' said Shadow.

'He really is a good boy,' said the bald young man's mother, and she led her son by the sleeve, into the corridor and away, trailing a tag of toilet paper.

Shadow walked out into the hall. 'Excuse me,' he said. They turned, the man and his mother.

'You've got something on your shoe,' said Shadow.

She looked down. Then she stepped on the strip of paper with her other shoe, and lifted her foot, freeing it. She nodded at Shadow, approvingly, and walked away.

Shadow went to the reception desk. 'Gordon, have you got a good local map?'

'Like an Ordnance Survey? Absolutely. I'll bring it into the lounge for you.'

Shadow went back into the bar and finished his coffee. Gordon brought in a map. Shadow was impressed by the detail: it seemed to show every goat-track. He inspected it closely, tracing his walk. He found the hill where he had stopped and eaten his lunch. He ran his finger south-west. 'There aren't any castles around here, are there?'

'I'm afraid not. There are some to the east. I've got a guide to the castles of Scotland I could let you look at—'

'No, no. That's fine. Are there any big houses in this area? The kind people would call castles? Or big estates?'

'Well, there's the Cape Wrath Hotel, just over here,' and he pointed to it on the map. 'But it's a fairly empty area. Technically, for human occupation, what do they call it?, for population density, it's a desert up here. Not even any interesting ruins, I'm afraid. Not that you could walk to.'

Shadow thanked him, then asked him for an early-morning alarm call. He wished he had been able to find the house he had seen from the hill on the map, but perhaps he had been looking in the wrong place. It wouldn't be the first time.

The couple in the room next door were fighting, or making love. Shadow could not tell, but each time he began to drift off to sleep raised voices or cries would jerk him awake.

Later, he was never certain if it had really happened, if she had really come to him, or if it had been the first of that night's dreams, but in truth or in dreams, shortly before midnight by the bedside clock-radio, there was a knock on his bedroom door. He got up. Called, 'Who is it?'

'Jennie.'

He opened the door, winced at the light in the hall.

She was wrapped in her brown coat, and she looked up at him hesitantly.

'Yes?' said Shadow.

'You'll be going to the house tomorrow,' she said.

'Yes.'

'I thought I should say goodbye,' she said. 'In case I don't get a chance to see you again. And if you don't come back to the hotel. And you just go on somewhere. And I never see you.'

'Well, goodbye, then,' said Shadow.

She looked him up and down, examining the T-shirt and the boxers he slept in, at his bare feet, then up at his face. She seemed worried. 'You know where I live,' she said at last. 'Call me if you need me.'

She reached her index finger out and touched it gently to his lips. Her finger was very cold. Then she took a step back into the corridor and just stood there, facing him, making no move to go.

Shadow closed the hotel-room door, and he heard her foot steps walking away down the corridor. He climbed back into bed.

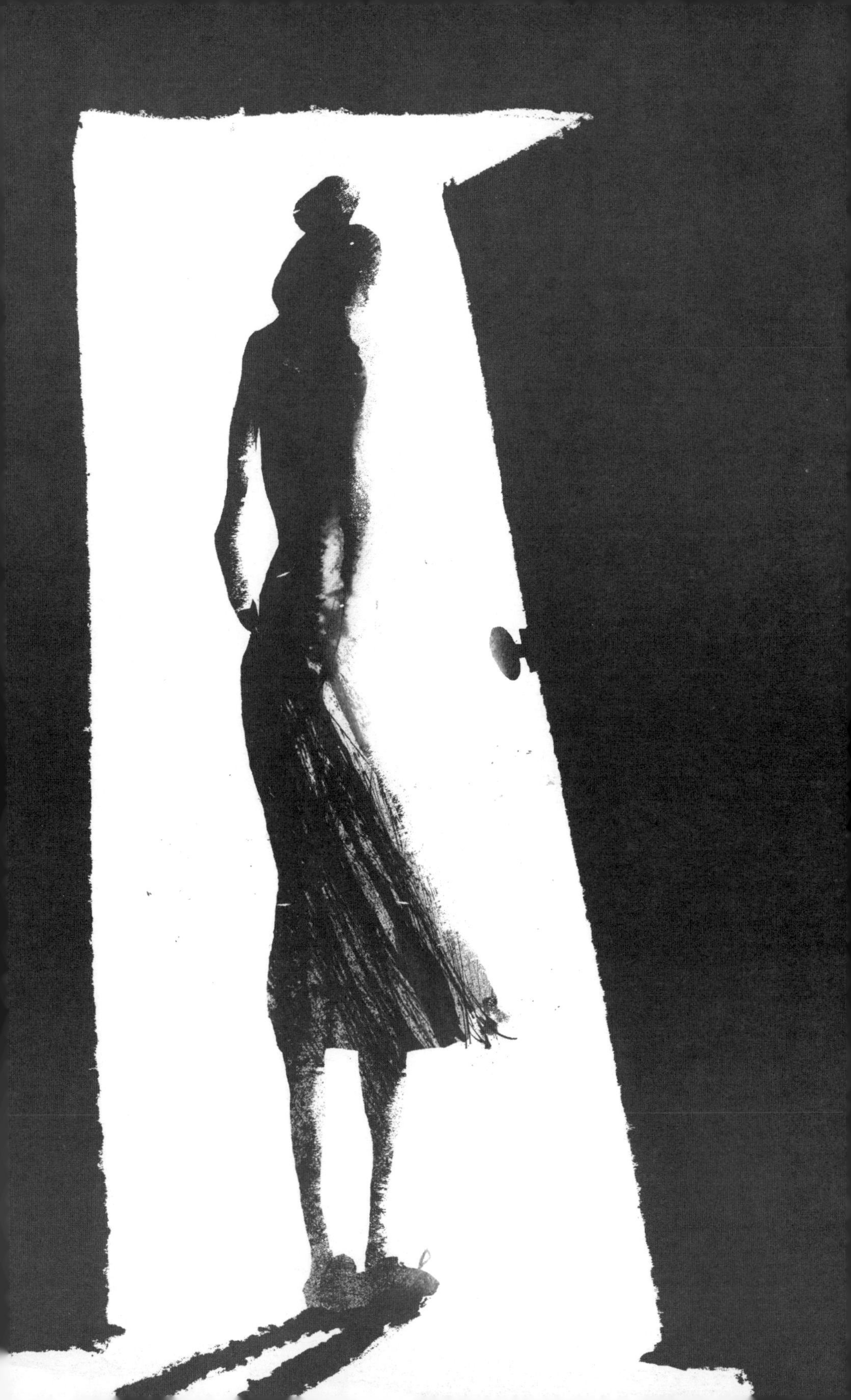

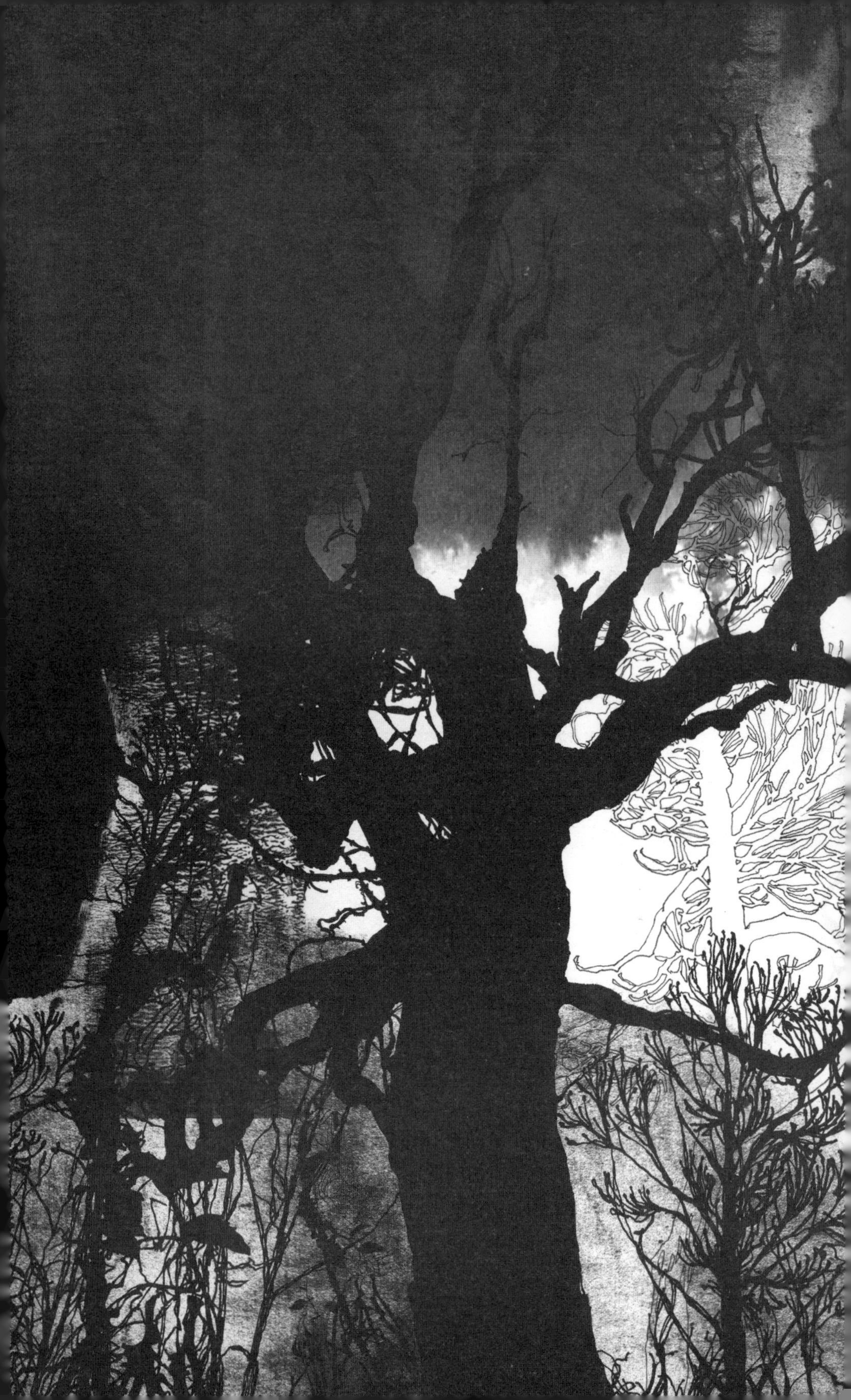

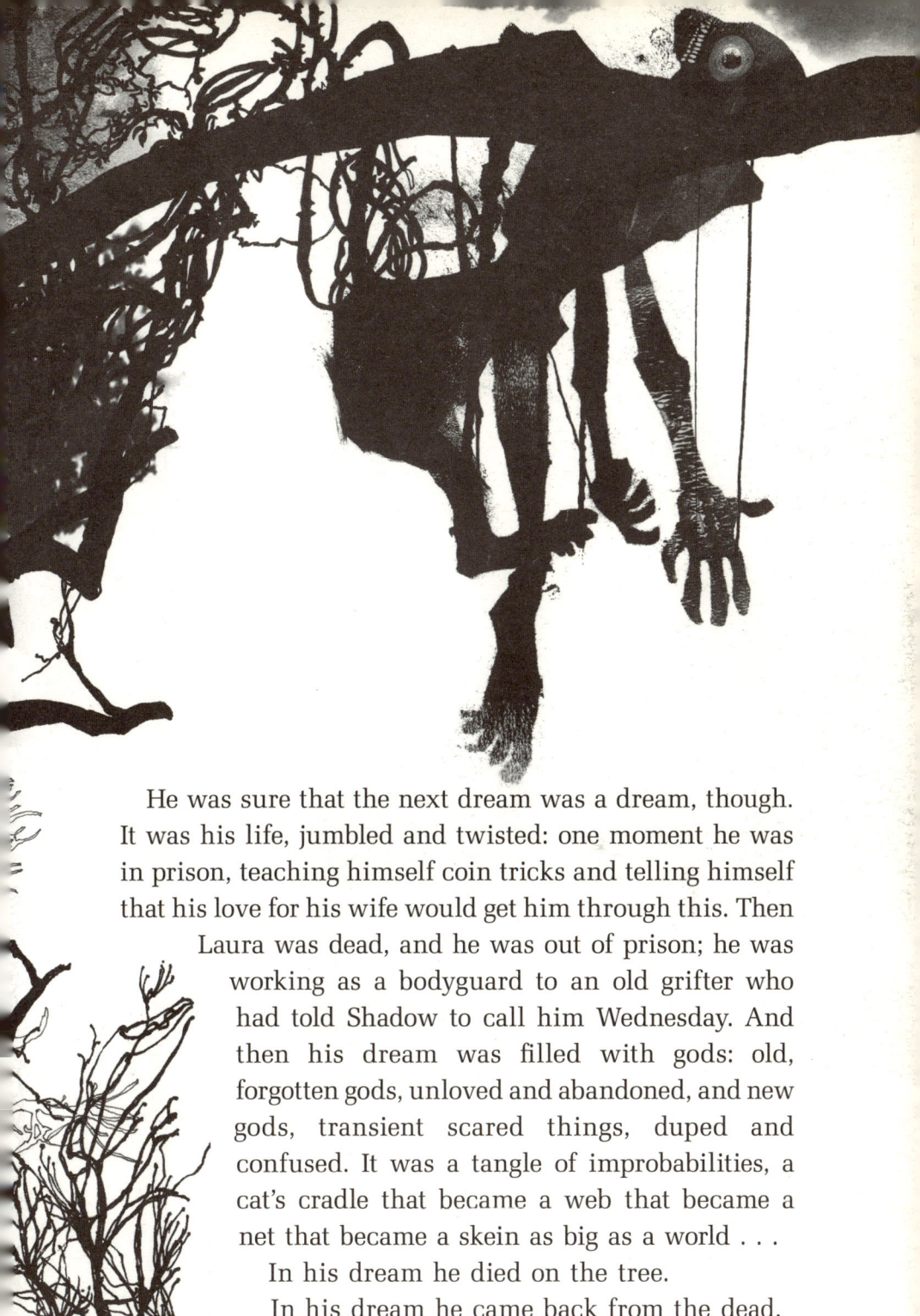

He was sure that the next dream was a dream, though. It was his life, jumbled and twisted: one moment he was in prison, teaching himself coin tricks and telling himself that his love for his wife would get him through this. Then Laura was dead, and he was out of prison; he was working as a bodyguard to an old grifter who had told Shadow to call him Wednesday. And then his dream was filled with gods: old, forgotten gods, unloved and abandoned, and new gods, transient scared things, duped and confused. It was a tangle of improbabilities, a cat's cradle that became a web that became a net that became a skein as big as a world . . .

In his dream he died on the tree.

In his dream he came back from the dead.

And after that there was darkness.

Mr Smith

IV

The telephone beside the bed shrilled at seven. He showered, shaved, dressed, packed his world into his backpack. Then he went down to the restaurant for breakfast: salty porridge, limp bacon and oily fried eggs. The coffee, though, was surprisingly good.

At ten past eight he was in the lobby, waiting.

At fourteen minutes past eight, a man came in, wearing a sheepskin coat. He was sucking on a hand-rolled cigarette. The man stuck out his hand, cheerfully. 'You'll be Mister Moon,' he said. 'My name's Smith. I'm your lift out to the big house.' The man's grip was firm. 'You *are* a big feller, aren't you?'

Unspoken was 'But I could take you,' although Shadow knew that it was there.

Shadow said, 'So they tell me. You aren't Scottish.'

'Not me, matey. Just up for the week to make sure that everything runs like it's s'posed to. I'm a London boy.' A flash of teeth in a hatchet-blade face. Shadow guessed that the man was in his mid-forties. 'Come on out to the car.

I can bring you up to speed on the way. Is that your bag?'

Shadow carried his backpack out to the car, a muddy Land-Rover, its engine still running. He dropped his bag in the back, climbed into the passenger seat. Smith pulled one final drag on his cigarette, now little more than a rolled stub of white paper, and threw it out of the open driver's-side window into the road.

They drove out of the village.

'So how do I pronounce your name?' asked Smith. 'Balder or Borl-der, or something else? Like Cholmondeley is actually pronounced Chumley.'

'Shadow,' said Shadow. 'People call me Shadow.'

'Right.'

Silence.

'So,' said Smith. 'Shadow. I don't know how much old Gaskell told you about the party this weekend.'

'A little.'

'Right, well, the most important thing to know is this. Anything that happens, you keep shtum about. Right? Whatever you see, people having a little bit of fun, you don't say nothing to anybody, even if you recognise them, if you take my meaning.'

'I don't recognise people,' said Shadow.

'That's the spirit. We're just here to make sure that everyone has a good time without being disturbed. They've come a long way for a nice weekend.'

'Got it,' said Shadow.

They reached the ferry to the cape. Smith parked the Land-Rover beside the road, took their bags, and locked the car.

On the other side of the ferry crossing, an identical Land-Rover waited. Smith unlocked it, threw their bags into the back, and started the car along the dirt track.

They turned off before they reached the lighthouse, drove for a while in silence down a dirt road that rapidly turned into a sheep track. Several times Shadow had to get out and open gates; he waited while the Land-Rover drove through, closed the gates behind them.

There were ravens in the fields and on the low stone walls, huge black birds that stared at Shadow with implacable eyes.

'So you were in the nick?' said Smith, suddenly.

'Sorry?'

'Prison. Pokey. Porridge. Other words beginning with a P, indicating poor food, no nightlife, inadequate toilet facilities and limited opportunities for travel.'

'Yeah.'

'You're not very chatty, are you?'

'I thought that was a virtue.'

'Point taken. Just conversation. The silence was getting on my nerves. You like it up here?'

'I guess. I've only been here for a few days.'

'Gives me the fucking willies. Too remote. I've been to parts of Siberia that felt more welcoming. You been to London yet? No? When you come down south I'll show you around. Great pubs. Real food. And there's all that tourist stuff you Americans like. Traffic's hell, though. At least up here we can drive. No bloody traffic-lights. There's this traffic-light at the bottom of Regent Street, I swear, you sit there for five minutes on a red light, then you get about ten seconds on a green light. Two cars max. Sodding ridiculous. They say it's the price we pay for progress. Right?'

'Yeah,' said Shadow. 'I guess.'

They were well off-road now, thumping and bumping along a scrubby valley, between two high hills. 'Your party guests,' said Shadow. 'Are they coming in by Land-Rover?'

'Nah. We've got helicopters. They'll be in in time for dinner tonight. Choppers in, then choppers out on Sunday evening'.

'Like living on an island.'

'I wish we were living on an island. Wouldn't get loony locals causing problems, would we? Nobody complains about the noise coming from the island next door.'

'You make a lot of noise at your party?'

'It's not my party, chum. I'm just a facilitator. Making sure that everything runs smoothly. But, yes, I understand that they can make a lot of noise when they put their minds to it.'

The grassy valley became a sheep path, the sheep path became a driveway running almost straight up a hill. A bend in the road, a sudden turn, and they were driving towards a house that Shadow recognised. Jennie had pointed to it yesterday, at lunch.

The house was old. He could see that at a glance. Parts of it seemed older than others: there was a wall on one wing of the building built out of grey rocks and stones, heavy and hard. That wall jutted into another, built of brown bricks. The roof, which covered the whole building, both wings, was a dark grey slate. The house looked out on to a gravel drive, and then down the hill on to the loch. Shadow climbed out of the Land-Rover. He looked at the house and felt small. He felt as though he were coming home, and it was not a good feeling.

There were several other four-wheel-drive vehicles parked on the gravel. 'The keys to the cars are hanging in the pantry, in case you need to take one out. I'll show you as we go past.'

Through a large wooden door, and now they were in a central courtyard, partly paved. There was a small fountain in the middle of the courtyard, and a plot of grass, a ragged green, viperous swath bounded by grey flagstones.

'This is where the Saturday-night action will be,' said Smith. 'I'll show you where you'll be staying.'

Into the smaller wing through an unimposing door, past a room hung with keys on hooks, each key marked with a paper tag, and another room filled with empty shelves. Down a dingy hall, and up some stairs. There was no carpeting on the stairs, nothing but whitewash on the walls. ('Well, this is the servants' quarters, innit? They never spent any money on it.') It was cold, in a way that Shadow was starting to become familiar with: colder inside the building than out. He wondered how they did that, if it was a British building secret.

Smith led Shadow to the top of the house, and showed him into a dark room containing an antique wardrobe, an iron-framed single bed that Shadow could see at a glance would be smaller than he was, an ancient washstand, and a small window that looked out on to the inner courtyard.

'There's a loo at the end of the hall,' said Smith. 'The servants' bathroom's on the next floor down. Two baths, one for men, one for women, no showers. The supplies of hot water on this wing of the house are distinctly limited, I'm afraid. Your monkey-suit's hanging in the wardrobe. Try it on now, see if it all fits, then leave it off until this evening, when the guests come in. Limited dry-cleaning facilities. We might as well be on Mars. I'll be down in the kitchen if you need me. It's not as cold down there, if the Aga's working. Bottom of the stairs and left, then right, then yell if you're lost. Don't go into the other wing unless you're told to.'

He left Shadow alone.

Shadow tried on the black tuxedo jacket, the white dress shirt, the black tie. There were highly polished black shoes as well. It all fitted, as if it had been tailored for him. He hung everything back in the wardrobe.

He walked down the stairs, found Smith on the landing, stabbing angrily at a small silver mobile phone. 'No bloody reception. The thing rang, now I'm trying to call back it won't give me a signal. It's the bloody stone age up here. How was your suit? All right?'

'Perfect.'

'That's my boy. Never use five words if you can get away with one, eh? I've known dead men talk more than you do.'

'Really?'

'Nah. Figure of speech. Come on. Fancy some lunch?'

'Sure. Thank you.'

'Right. Follow me. It's a bit of a warren, but you'll get the hang of it soon enough.'

They ate in the huge, empty kitchen: Shadow and Smith piled enamelled tin plates with slices of translucent orange smoked salmon on crusty white bread, and slices of sharp cheese, accompanied by mugs of strong, sweet tea. The Aga was, Shadow discovered, a big metal box, part oven, part water-heater. Smith opened one of the many doors on its side and shovelled in several large scoops of coal.

'So where's the rest of the food? And the waiters, and the cooks?' asked Shadow. 'It can't just be us.'

'Well spotted. Everything's coming up from Edinburgh. It'll run like clockwork. Food and party workers will be here at three, and unpack. Guests get brought in at six. Buffet dinner is served at eight. Talk a lot, eat, have a bit of a laugh, nothing too strenuous. Tomorrow there's breakfast from seven to midday. Guests get to go for walks, scenic views and all that in the afternoon. Bonfires are built in the courtyard. Then in the evening the bonfires are lit, everybody has a wild Saturday night in the north, hopefully without being bothered by our neighbours. Sunday morning we tiptoe around, out of respect for everybody's hangover, Sunday afternoon the choppers land and we wave everybody on their way. You collect your pay packet, and I'll drive you back to the hotel, or you can ride south with me, if you fancy a change. Sounds good?'

'Sounds just dandy,' said Shadow. 'And the folks who may show up on the Saturday night?'

'Just killjoys. Locals out to ruin everybody's good time.'

'What locals?' asked Shadow. 'There's nothing but sheep for miles.'

'Locals. They're all over the place,' said Smith. 'You just don't see them. Tuck themselves away like Sawney Beane and his family.'

Shadow said, 'I think I've heard of him. The name rings a bell . . .'

'He's *historical*,' said Smith. He slurped his tea, and leaned back in his chair. 'This was, what?, six hundred years back – after the Vikings had buggered off back to Scandinavia, or intermarried and converted until they were just another bunch of Scots, but before Queen Elizabeth died and James came down from Scotland to rule both countries. Somewhere in there.' He took a swig of his tea. 'So. Travellers in Scotland kept vanishing. It wasn't that unusual. I mean, if you set out on a long journey back then, you didn't always get home. Sometimes it would be months before anyone knew you weren't coming home again, and they'd blame the wolves or the weather, and resolve to travel in groups, and only in the summer.

'One traveller, though, he was riding with a bunch of companions through a glen, and there came over the hill, dropped from the trees, up from the ground, a swarm, a flock, a pack of children, armed with daggers and knives

and bone clubs and stout sticks, and they pulled the travellers off their horses, and fell on them, and finished them off. All but this one geezer, and he was riding a little behind the others, and he got away. He was the only one, but it only takes one, doesn't it? He made it to the nearest town, and raised the hue and cry, and they gather a troop of townsfolk and soldiers and they go back there, with dogs.

'It takes them days to find the hideout, they're ready to give up when, at the mouth of a cave by the seashore, the dogs start to howl. And they go down.

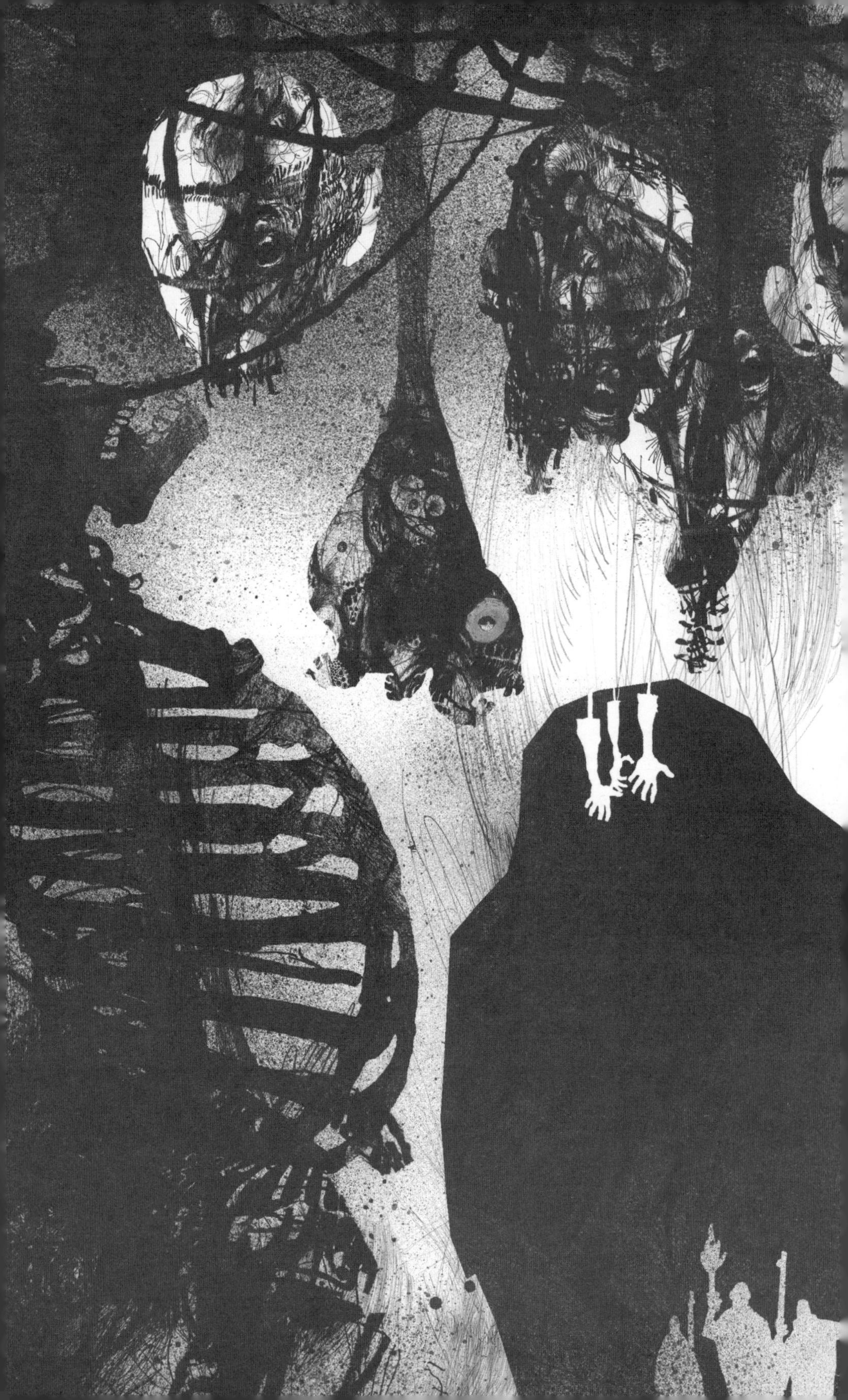

'Turns out there's caves, under the ground, and in the biggest and deepest of the caves is old Sawney Beane and his brood, and carcases, hanging from hooks, smoked and slow-roast. Legs, arms, thighs, hands and feet of men, women and children are hung up in rows, like dried pork. There are limbs pickled in brine, like salt beef. There's money in heaps, gold and silver, with watches, rings, swords, pistols and clothes, riches beyond imagining, as they never spent a single penny of it. Just stayed in their caves, and ate, and bred, and hated.

'He'd been living there for years. King of his own little kingdom, was old Sawney, him and his wife, and their children and grandchildren, and some of those grandchildren were also their children. An incestuous little bunch.'

'Did this really happen?'

'So I'm told. There are court records. They took the family to Leith to be tried. The court decision was interesting – they decided that Sawney Beane, by virtue of his acts, had removed himself from the human race. So they sentenced him as an animal. They didn't hang him or behead him. They just got a big fire going and threw the Beanies on to it, to burn to death.'

'All of his family?'

'I don't remember. They may have burned the little kids, or they may not. Probably did. They tend to deal very efficiently with monsters in this part of the world.'

Smith washed their plates and mugs in the sink, left them in a rack to dry. The two men walked out into the courtyard. Smith rolled himself a cigarette expertly. He licked the paper, smoothed it with his fingers, lit the finished tube with a Zippo. 'Let's see. What d'you need to know for tonight? Well, basics are easy: speak when you're spoken to – not that you're going to find that one a problem, eh?'

Shadow said nothing.

'Right. If one of the guests asks you for something, do your best to provide it, ask me if you're in any doubt, but do what the guests ask as long as it doesn't take you off what you're doing, or violate the prime directive.'

'Which is?'

'Don't. Shag. The posh totty. There's sure to be some young ladies who'll take it into their heads, after half a bottle of wine, that what they really need is a bit of rough. And if that happens, you do a *Sunday People*.'

'I have no idea what you're talking about.'

'*Our reporter made his excuses and left*. Yes? You can look, but you can't touch. Got it?'

'Got it.'

'Smart boy.'

Shadow found himself starting to like Smith. He told himself that liking this man was not a sensible thing to do. He had met people like Smith before, people without consciences, without scruples, without hearts, and they were uniformly as dangerous as they were likeable.

In the early afternoon the servants arrived, brought in by a helicopter that looked like a troop carrier; they unpacked boxes of wine and crates of food, hampers and containers with astonishing efficiency. There were boxes filled with napkins and with tablecloths. There were cooks and waiters, waitresses and chambermaids.

But first off the helicopter there were the security guards: big, solid men with earpieces and what Shadow had no doubt were gun-bulges beneath their jackets. They reported one by one to Smith, who set them to inspecting the house and the grounds.

Shadow was helping out, carrying boxes filled with vegetables from the chopper to the kitchen. He could carry twice as much as anyone else. The next time he passed Smith he stopped and said, 'So, if you've got all these security guys, what am I here for?'

Smith smiled affably. 'Look, son. There's people coming to this do who're worth more than you or I will ever see in a lifetime. They need to be sure they'll be looked after. Kidnappings happen. People have enemies. Lots of things happen. Only with those lads around, they won't. But having them deal with grumpy locals, it's like setting a landmine to stop trespassers. Yeah?'

'Right,' said Shadow. He went back to the chopper, picked up another box marked 'baby aubergines' and filled with

small black
eggplants, put it on top
of a crate of cabbages and
carried them both to the
kitchen, certain now that he was
being lied to. Smith's reply was
reasonable. It was even convincing. It simply
wasn't true. There was no reason for him to be there, or
if there was it wasn't the reason he'd been given.

He chewed it over, trying to figure out why he was in that house, and hoped that he was showing nothing on the surface. Shadow kept it all on the inside. It was safer there.

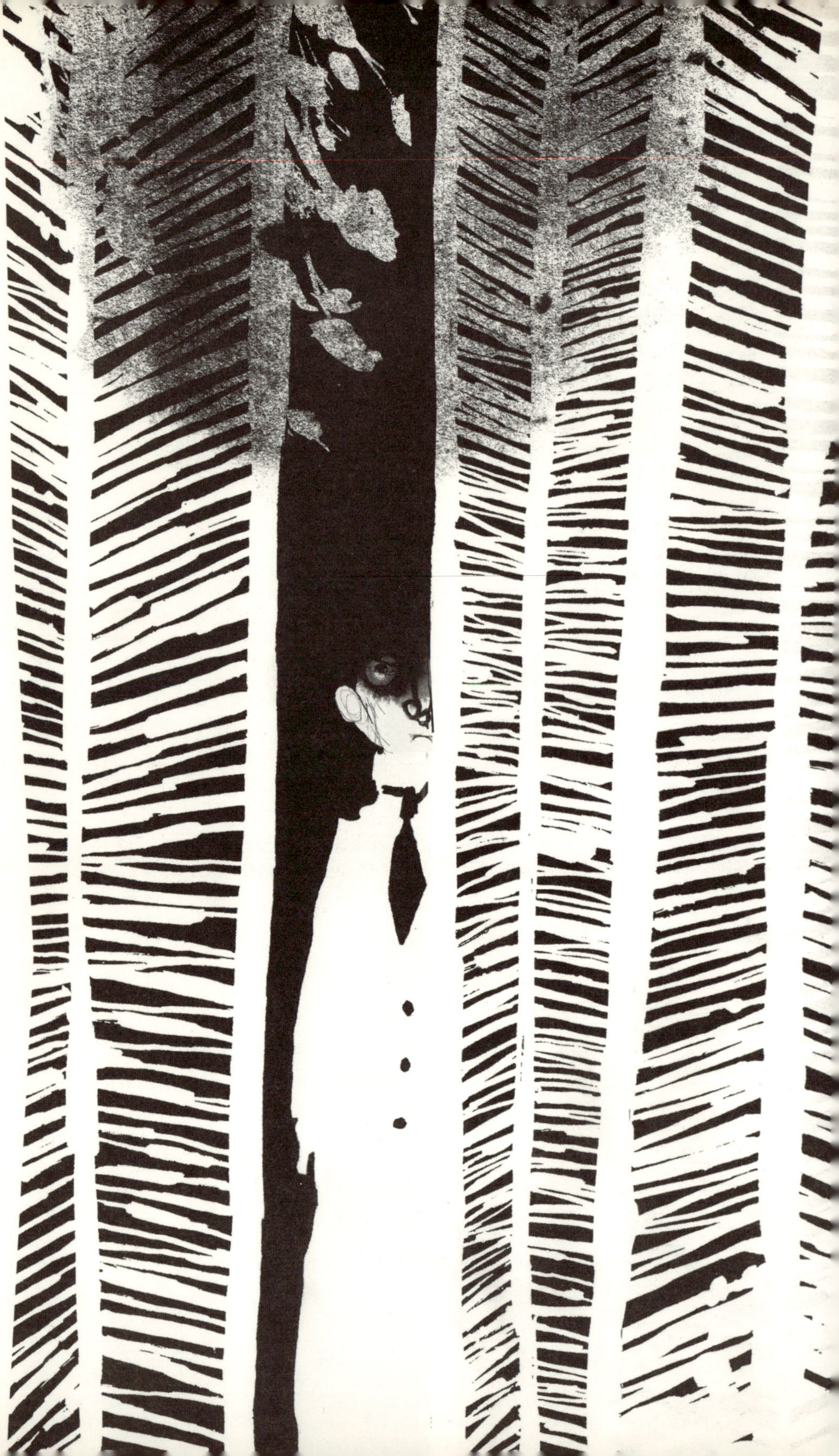

V

More helicopters came down in the early evening, as the sky was turning pink, and a score or more of smart people clambered out. Several of them were smiling and laughing. Most of them were in their thirties and forties. Shadow recognised none of them.

Smith moved casually but smoothly from person to person, greeting them confidently. 'Right, now you go through there and turn left, and wait in the main hall. Lovely big log fire there. Someone'll come and take you up to your room. Your luggage should be waiting for you there. You call me if it's not, but it will be. 'Ullo, your ladyship, you do look a treat – shall I 'ave someone carry your 'andbag? Looking forward to termorrer? Aren't we all.'

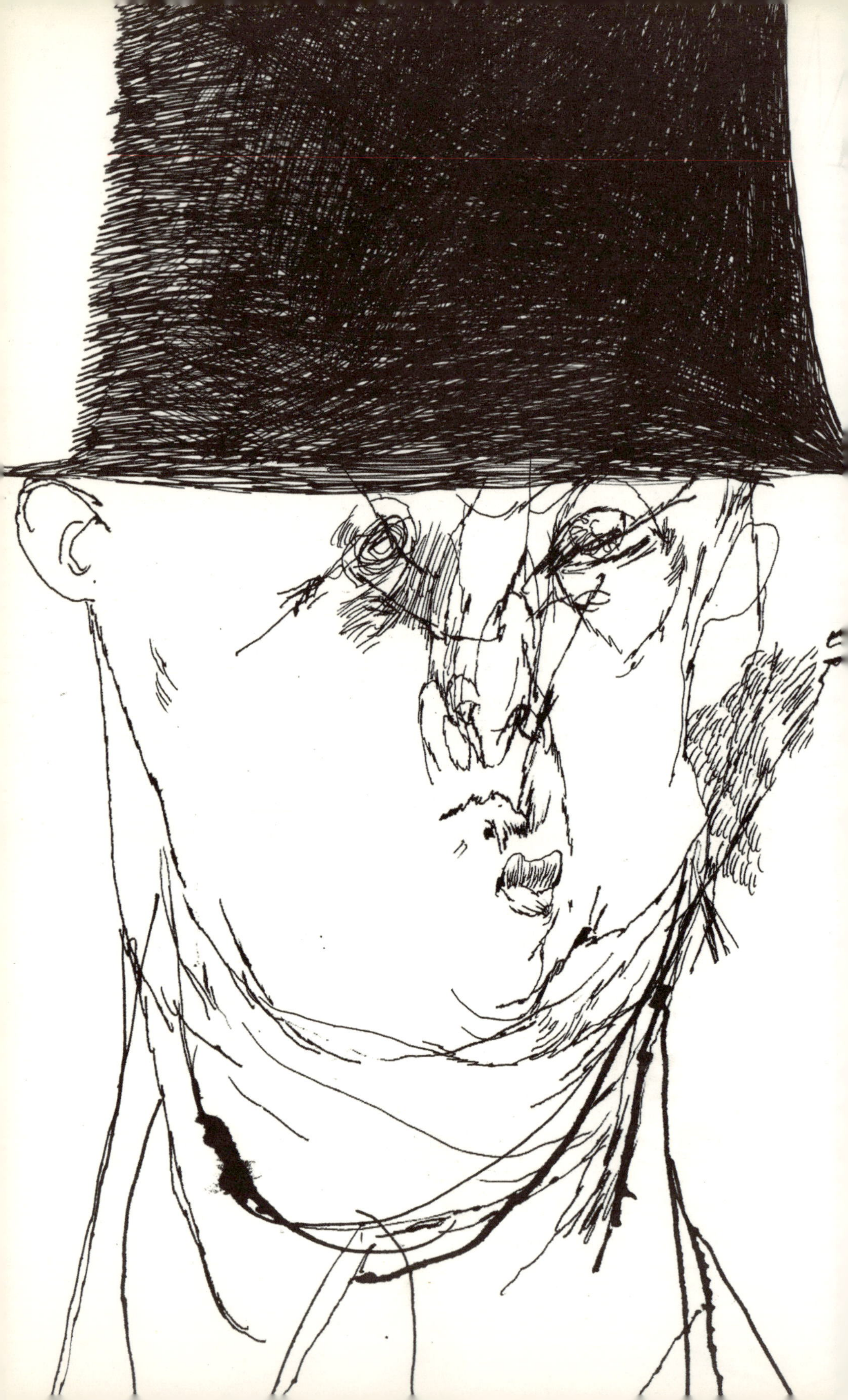

Shadow watched, fascinated, as Smith dealt with each of the guests, his manner an expert mixture of familiarity and deference, of amiability and Cockney charm: aitches, consonants and vowel sounds came and went and transformed according to who he was talking to.

A woman with short dark hair, very pretty, smiled at Shadow as he carried her bags inside. 'Posh totty,' muttered Smith, as he went past. 'Hands off.'

A portly man, whom Shadow estimated to be in his early sixties, was the last person off the chopper. He walked over to Smith, leaned on a cheap wooden walking-stick, said something in a low voice. Smith replied in the same fashion.

He's in charge, thought Shadow. It was there in the body language. Smith was no longer smiling, no longer cajoling. He was reporting, efficiently and quietly, telling the old man everything he should know.

Smith crooked a finger at Shadow, who walked quickly over to them.

'Shadow,' said Smith, 'this is Mister Alice.'

Mr Alice put out his hand, shook Shadow's big, dark hand with his pink, pudgy one. 'Great pleasure to meet you,' he said. 'Heard good things about you.'

'Good to meet you,' said Shadow.

'Well,' said Mr Alice, 'carry on.'

Smith nodded at Shadow, a gesture of dismissal.

'If it's okay by you,' said Shadow to Smith, 'I'd like to take a look around while there's still some light. Get a sense of where the locals could come from.'

'Don't go too far,' said Smith. He picked up Mr Alice's briefcase, and led the older man into the building.

Shadow walked the outside perimeter of the house. He had been set up. He did not know why, but he knew he was right. There was too much that didn't add up. Why hire a drifter to do security, while bringing in real security guards? It made no sense, no more than Smith introducing him to Mr Alice, after two dozen other people had treated Shadow as no more human than a decorative ornament.

There was a low stone wall in front of the house. Behind the house, a hill that was almost a small mountain; in front of it, a gentle slope down to the loch. Off to the side was the track by which he had arrived that morning. He walked to the far side of the house, and found what seemed to be a kitchen garden, with a high stone wall and wilderness beyond. He took a step down into the kitchen garden, and walked over to inspect the wall.

'You doing a recce, then?' said one of the security guards, in his black tuxedo. Shadow had not seen him there, which meant, he supposed, that he was very good at his job. Like most of the servants, his accent was Scottish.

'Just having a look around.'

'Get the lay of the land, very wise. Don't you worry about this side of the house. A hundred yards that way there's a river leads down to the loch, and beyond that just wet rocks for a hundred feet or so, straight down. Absolutely treacherous.'

'Oh. So the locals, the ones who come and complain, where do they come from?'

'I wouldnae have a clue.'

'I should head on over there and take a look at it,' said Shadow. 'See if I can figure out the ways in and out.'

'I wouldnae do that,' said the guard. 'Not if I were you. It's really treacherous. You go poking around over there, one slip, you'll be crashing down the rocks into the loch. They'll never find your body, if you head out that way.'

'I see,' said Shadow, who did.

He kept walking around the house. He spotted five other security guards, now that he was looking for them. He was sure there were others that he had missed.

In the main wing of the house he could see, through the french windows, a huge, wood-panelled dining room, and the guests seated around a table, talking and laughing.

He walked back into the servants' wing. As each course was done with, the serving plates were put out on a sideboard, and the staff helped themselves, piling food high on paper plates. Smith was sitting at the wooden kitchen table, tucking into a plate of salad and rare beef.

'There's caviar over there,' he said to Shadow. 'It's Golden Osetra, top quality, very special. What the party officials used to keep for themselves in the old days. I've never been a fan of the stuff, but help yourself.'

Shadow put a little of the caviar on the side of his plate, to be polite. He took some tiny boiled eggs, some pasta and some chicken. He sat next to Smith, and started to eat. 'I don't see where your locals are going to come from,' he said. 'Your men have the drive sealed off. Anyone who wants to come here would have to come over the loch.'

'You had a good poke around, then?'

'Yes,' said Shadow.

'You met some of my boys?'

'Yes.'

'What did you think?'

'I wouldn't want to mess with them.'

Smith smirked. 'Big fellow like you? You could take care of yourself.'

'They're killers,' said Shadow, simply.

'Only when they need to be,' said Smith. He was no longer smiling. 'Why don't you stay up in your room? I'll give you a shout when I need you.'

'Sure,' said Shadow. 'And if you don't need me, this is going to be a very easy weekend.'

Smith stared at him. 'You'll earn your money,' he said.

Shadow went up the back stairs to the long corridor at the top of the house. He went into his room. He could hear party noises, and looked out of the small window. The french windows opposite were wide open, and the partygoers, now wearing coats and gloves, holding their glasses of wine, had spilled out into the inner courtyard. He could hear fragments of conversations that transformed and reshaped themselves; the noises were clear but the words and the sense were lost. An occasional phrase would break free of the susurrus. A man said, 'I told him, judges like you, I don't own, I sell . . .' Shadow heard a woman say, 'It's a monster, darling. An absolute monster. Well, what can you do?' and another woman saying, 'Well, if only I could say the same about my boyfriend's!' and a bray of laughter.

He had two alternatives. He could stay, or he could try to go.

'I'll stay,' he said, aloud.

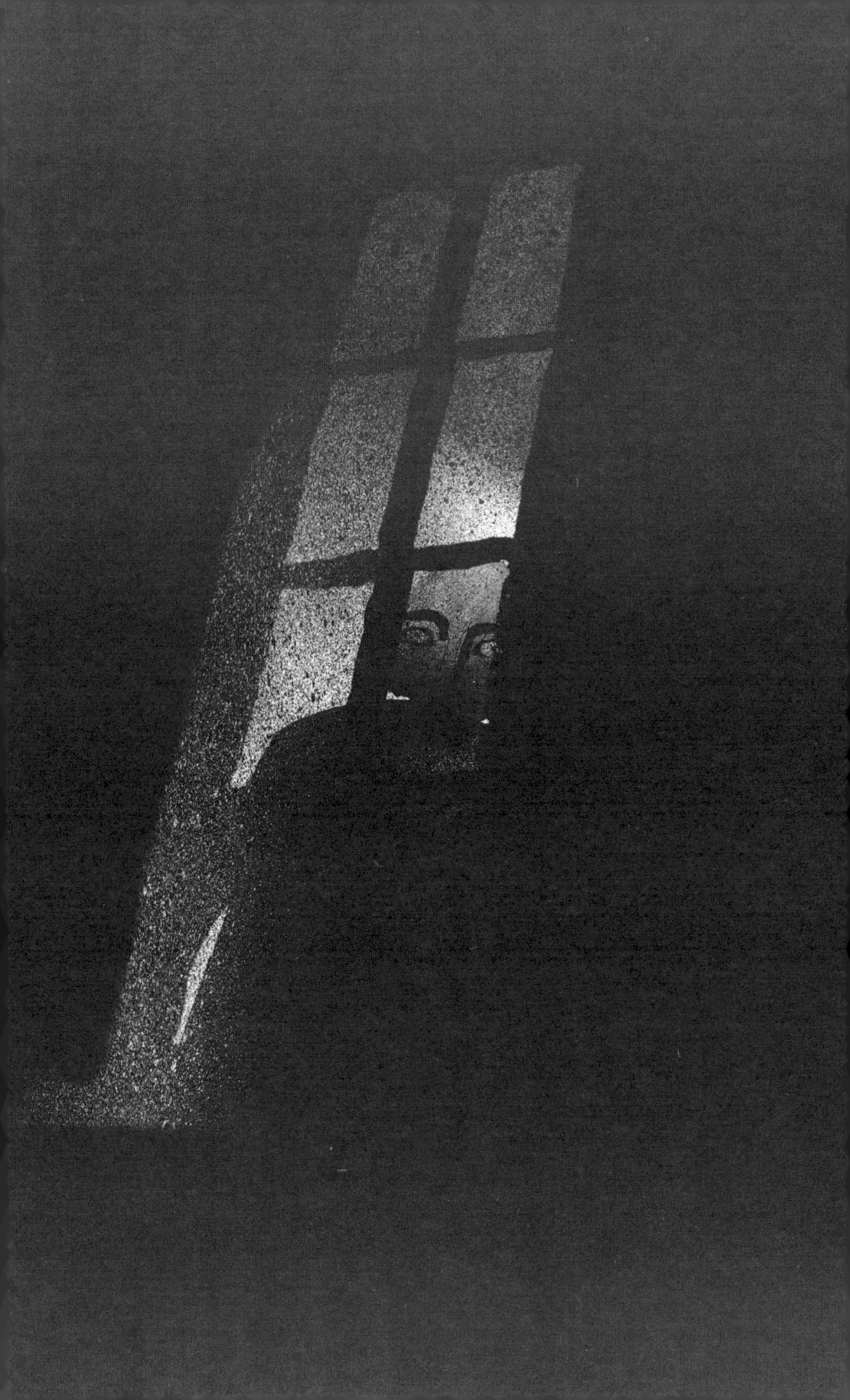

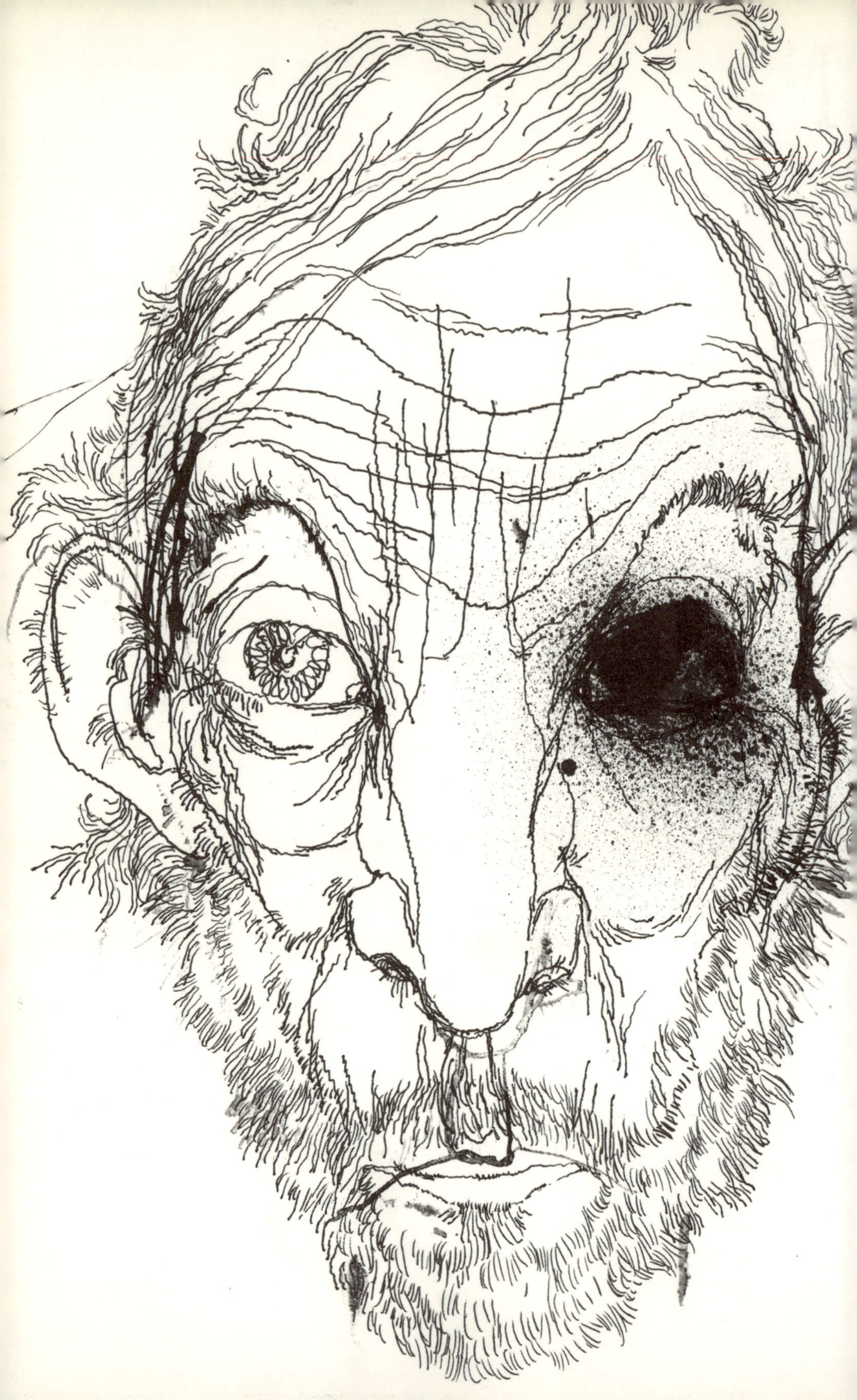

Mr Wednesday

VI

It was a night of dangerous dreams.

In Shadow's first dream he was back in America, standing beneath a streetlight. He walked up some steps, pushed through a glass door, and stepped into a diner, the kind that had once been a dining car on a train. He could hear an old man singing, in a deep gravelly voice, to the tune of 'My Bonnie Lies Over the Ocean':

> 'My grandpa sells condoms to sailors,
> He punctures the tips with a pin,
> My grandma does back-street abortions,
> My God how the money rolls in.'

Shadow walked along the length of the dining car. At a table at the end of the car, a grizzled man was sitting, holding a beer bottle, and singing, 'Rolls in, rolls in, my God how the money rolls in'. When he caught sight of Shadow his face split into a huge monkey grin, and he gestured with the beer bottle. 'Sit down, sit down,' he said.

Shadow sat down opposite the man he had known as Wednesday.

'So what's the trouble?' asked Wednesday, dead for almost two years, or as dead as his kind of creature was going to get. 'I'd offer you a beer, but the service here stinks.'

Shadow said that was okay. He didn't want a beer.

'Well?' asked Wednesday, scratching his beard.

'I'm in a big house in Scotland with a shitload of really rich folks, and they have an agenda. I'm in trouble, and I don't know what kind of trouble I'm in. But I think it's pretty bad trouble.'

Wednesday took a swig of his beer. 'The rich are different, m'boy,' he said, after a while.

'What the hell does *that* mean?'

'Well,' said Wednesday, 'for a start, most of them are probably mortal. Not something *you* have to worry about.'

'Don't give me that shit.'

'But you *aren't* mortal,' said Wednesday. 'You died on the tree, Shadow. You died and you came back.'

'So? I don't even remember how I did that. If they kill me this time, I'll still be dead.'

Wednesday finished his beer. Then he waved his beer bottle around, as if he were conducting an invisible orchestra with it, and sang another verse:

'My brother's a missionary worker,
He saves fallen women from sin,
For five bucks he'll save you a redhead,
My God how the money rolls in.'

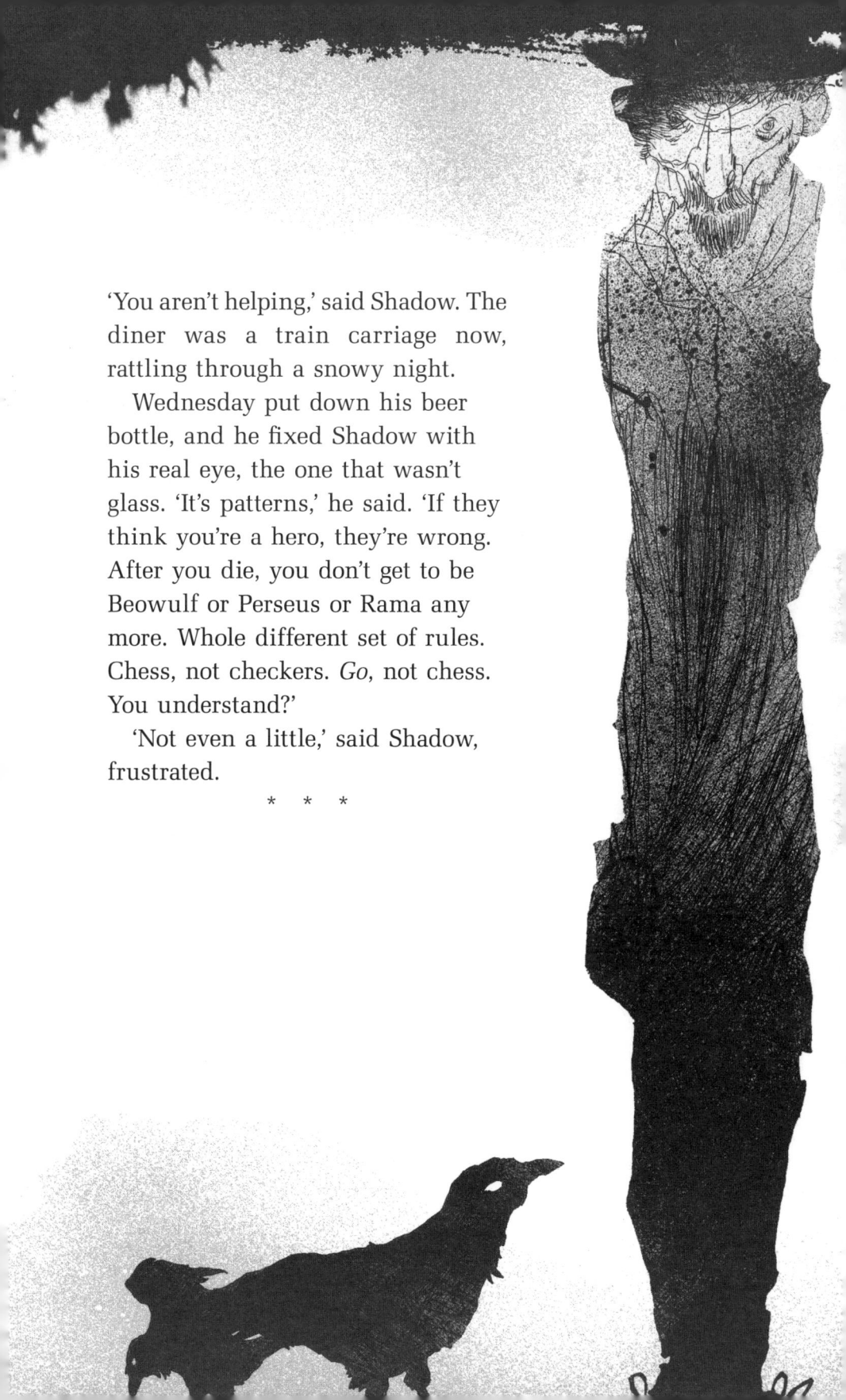

'You aren't helping,' said Shadow. The diner was a train carriage now, rattling through a snowy night.

Wednesday put down his beer bottle, and he fixed Shadow with his real eye, the one that wasn't glass. 'It's patterns,' he said. 'If they think you're a hero, they're wrong. After you die, you don't get to be Beowulf or Perseus or Rama any more. Whole different set of rules. Chess, not checkers. *Go*, not chess. You understand?'

'Not even a little,' said Shadow, frustrated.

* * *

People, in the corridor of the big house, moving loudly and drunkenly, shushing each other as they stumbled and giggled their way down the hall.

Shadow wondered if they were servants, or if they were strays from the other wing, slumming. And the dreams took him once again . . .

Now he was back in the bothy where he had sheltered from the rain the day before. There was a body on the floor: a boy, no more than five years old. Naked, on his back, limbs spread. There was a flash of intense light, and someone pushed through Shadow as if he was not there and rearranged the position of the boy's arms. Another flash of light.

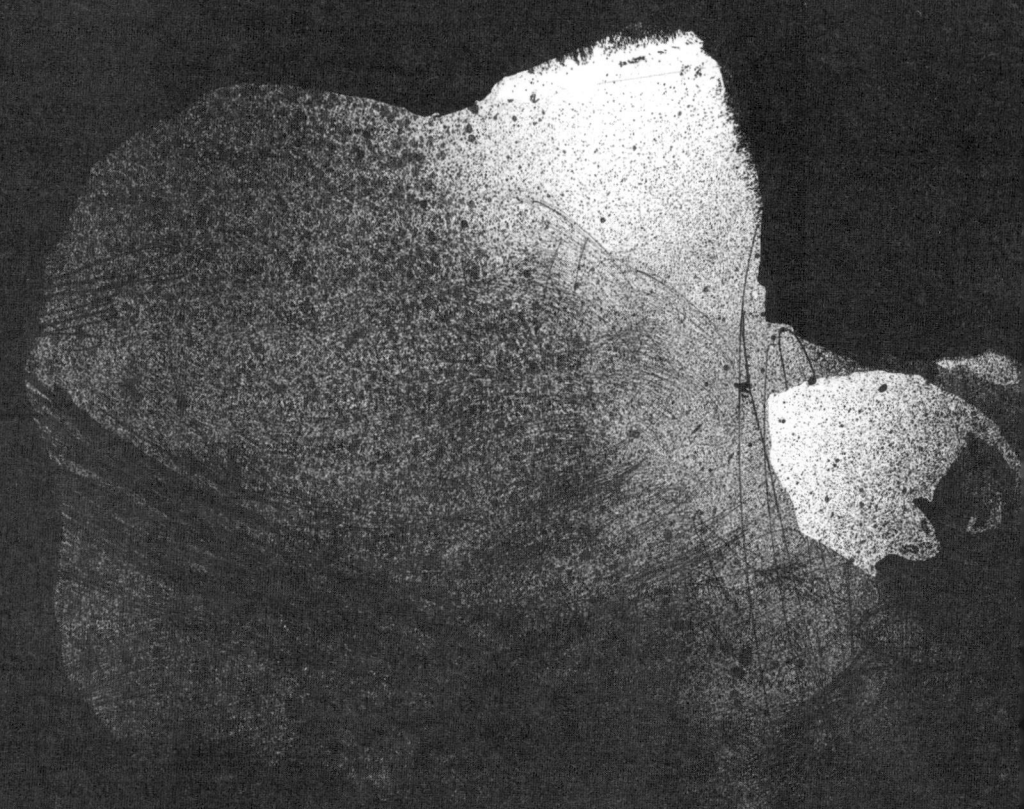

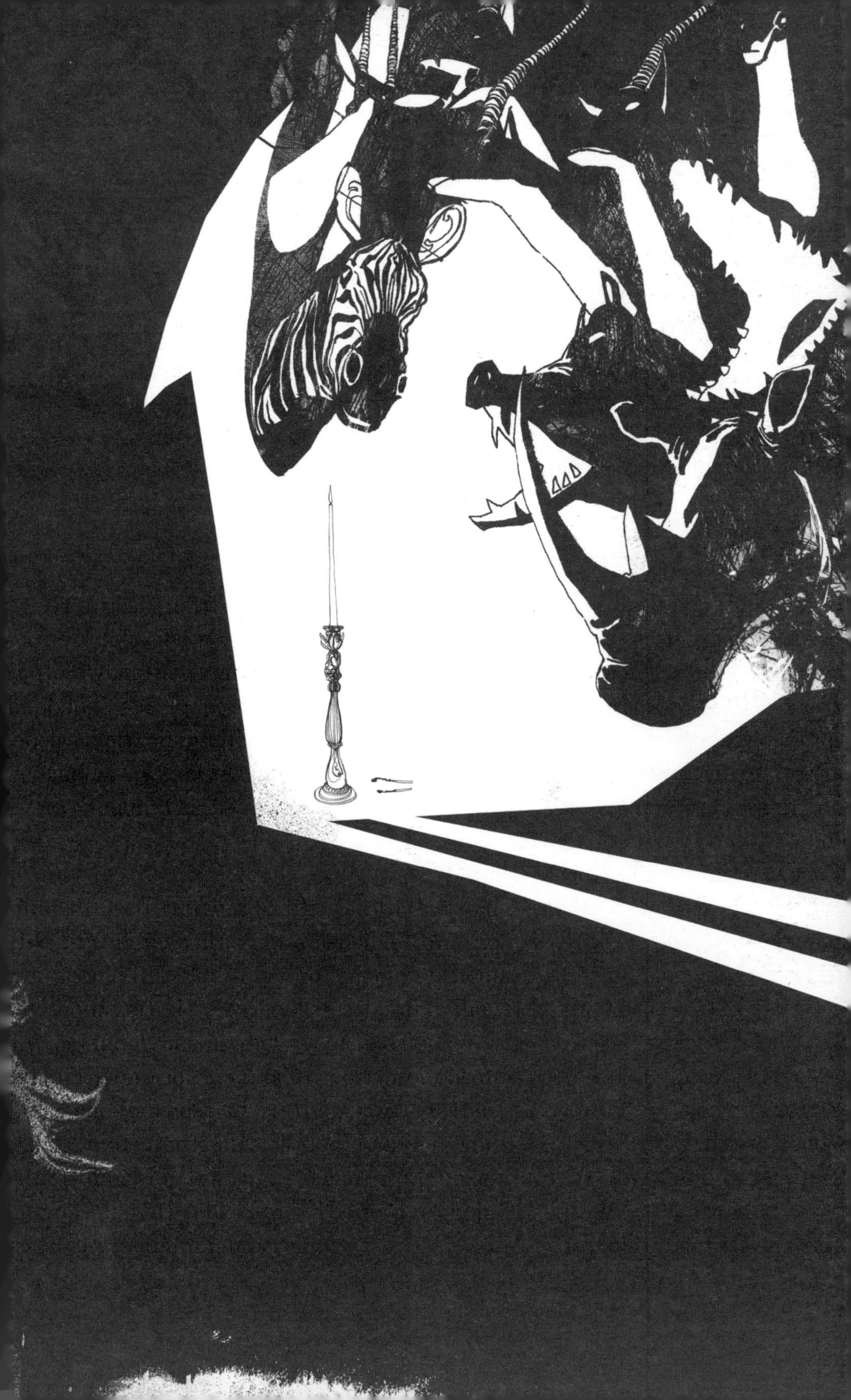

Shadow knew the man taking the photographs. It was Dr Gaskell, the little steel-haired man from the hotel bar.

Gaskell took a white-paper bag from his pocket, and fished about in it for something that he popped into his mouth. 'Dolly mixtures,' he said to the child on the stone floor. 'Yum yum. Your favourites.' He smiled and crouched down, and took another photograph of the dead boy.

Shadow pushed through the stone wall of the cottage, flowing through the cracks in the stones like the wind. He flowed down to the seashore. The waves crashed on the rocks and Shadow kept moving across the water, through grey seas, up the swells and down again, towards the ship made of dead men's nails.

The ship was far away, out at sea, and Shadow passed across the surface of the water like the shadow of a cloud.

The ship was huge. He had not understood before how huge it was. A hand reached down and grasped his hand, pulled him up from the sea on to the deck.

'Bring us back,' said a voice as loud as the crashing of the sea, urgent and fierce. 'Bring us back, or let us go.' Only one eye burned in that bearded face.

'I'm not keeping you here.'

They were giants, on that ship, huge men made of shadows and frozen sea-spray, creatures of dream and foam.

One of them, huger than all the rest, red-bearded, stepped forward. 'We cannot land,' he boomed. 'We cannot leave.'

'Go home,' said Shadow.

'We came with our people to this southern country,' said the one-eyed man. 'But they left us. They sought other, tamer gods, and they renounced us in their hearts, and gave us over.'

'Go home,' repeated Shadow.

'Too much time has passed,' said the red-bearded man. By the hammer at his side, Shadow knew him. 'Too much blood has been spilled. You are of our blood, Baldur. Set us free.'

And Shadow wanted to say that he was not theirs, was not anybody's, but the thin blanket had slipped from the bed, and his feet stuck out at the bottom, and thin moonlight filled the attic room.

There was silence, now, in that huge house. Something howled in the hills, and Shadow shivered.

He lay in a bed that was too small for him, and imagined time as something that pooled and puddled, wondered if there were places where time hung heavy, places where it was heaped and held – cities, he thought, must be filled with time: all the places where people congregated, where they came and brought time with them.

And if that were true, Shadow mused, then there could be other places, where the people were thin on the ground, and the land waited, bitter and granite, and a thousand years was an eyeblink to the hills – a scudding of clouds, a wavering of rushes, and nothing more, in the places where time was as thin on the ground as the people . . .

'They are going to kill you,' whispered Jennie, the barmaid.

Shadow sat beside her now, on the hill, in the moonlight. 'Why would they want to do that?' he asked. 'I don't matter.'

'It's what they do to monsters,' she said. 'It's what they have to do. It's what they've always done.'

He reached out to touch her, but she turned away from him. From behind, she was empty and hollow. She turned again, so she was facing him. 'Come away,' she whispered.

'You can come to me,' he said.

'I can't,' she said. 'There are things in the way. The way there is hard, and it is guarded. But you can call. If you call me, I'll come.'

Then dawn came, and with it a cloud of midges from the boggy land at the foot of the hill. Jennie flicked at them with her tail, but it was no use: they descended on Shadow like a cloud, until he was breathing midges, his nose and mouth filling with the tiny crawling stinging things, and he was choking on the darkness . . .

He wrenched himself back into his bed and his body and his life, into wakefulness, his heart pounding in his chest, gulping for breath.

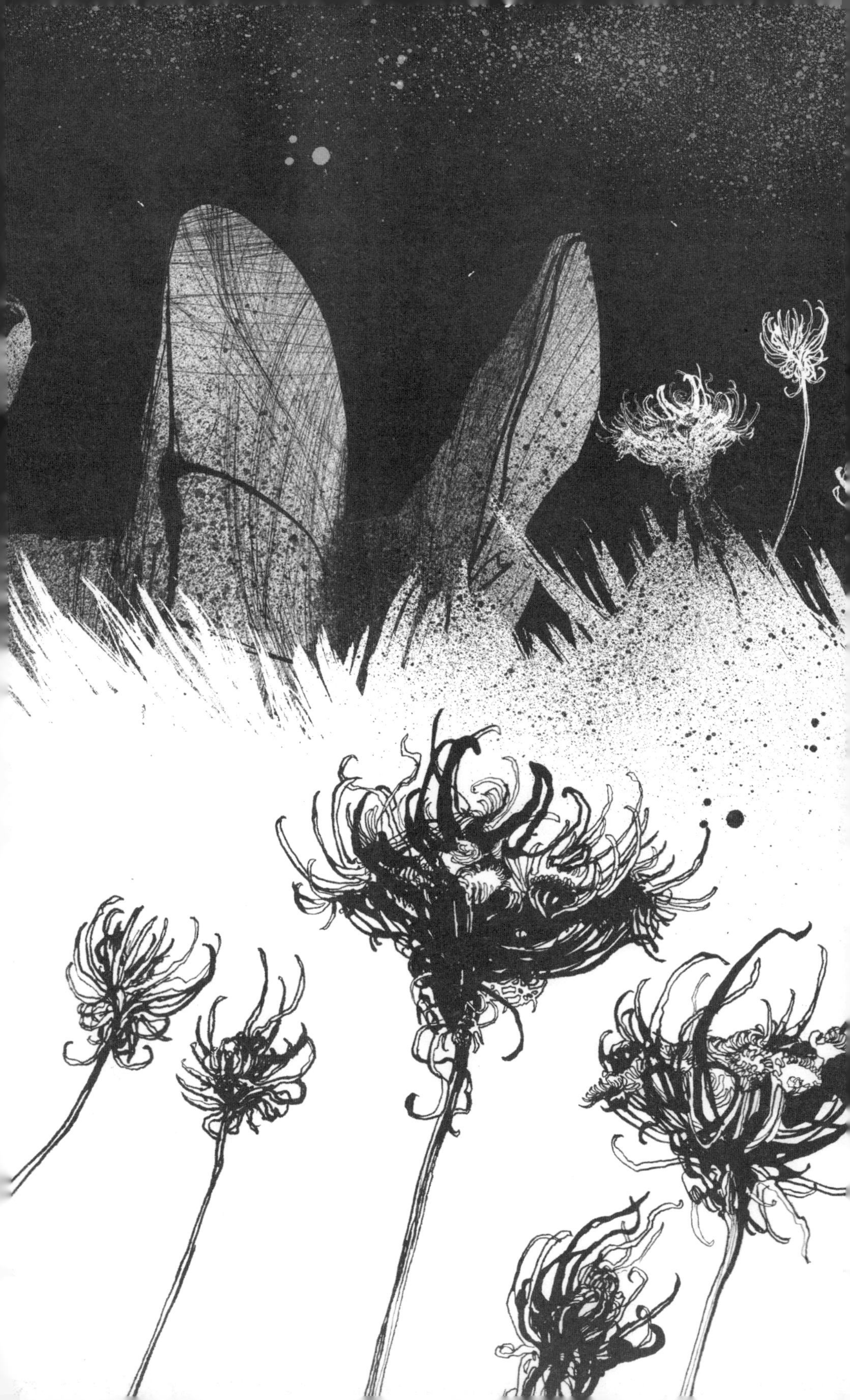

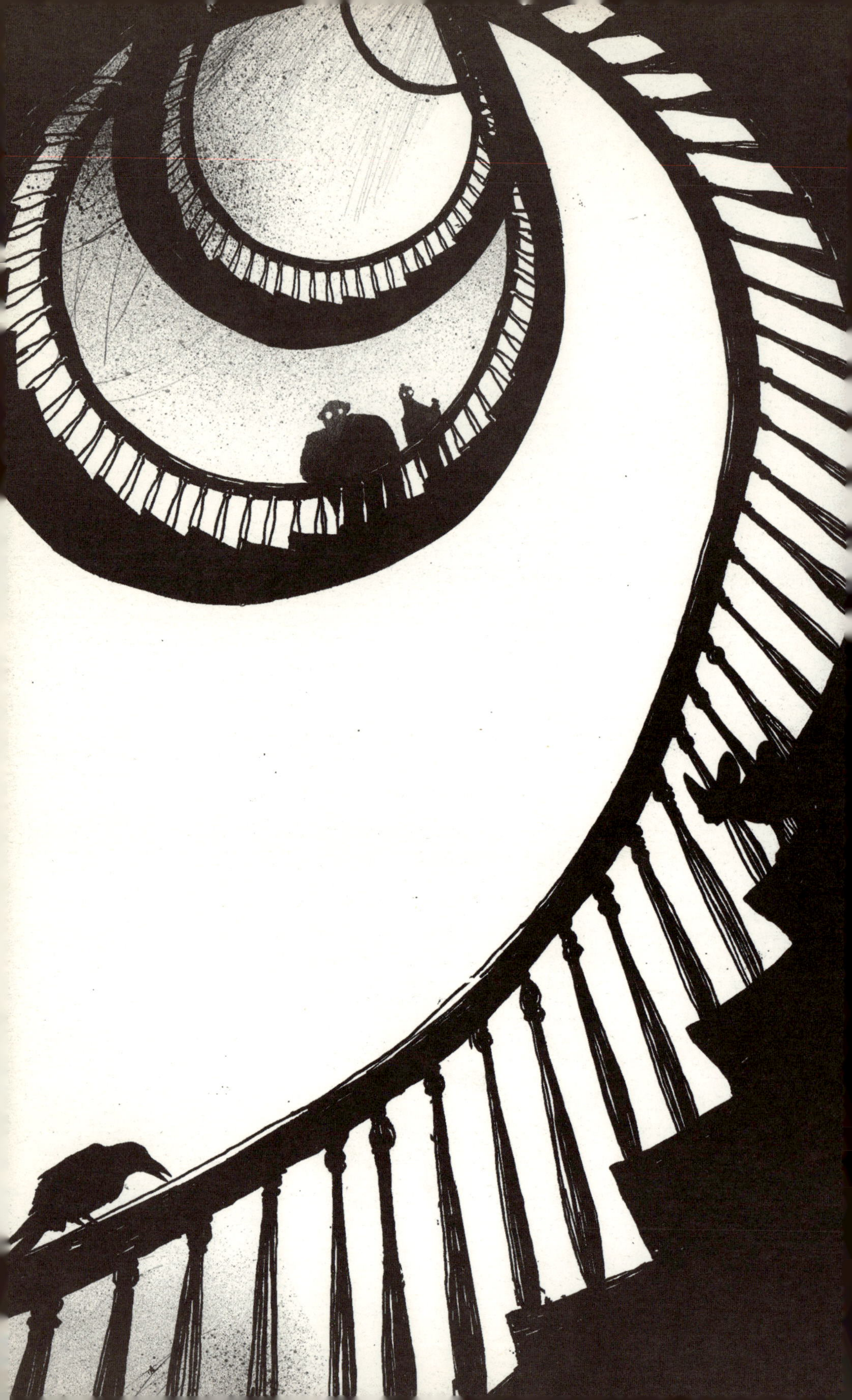

VII

Breakfast was kippers, grilled tomatoes, scrambled eggs, toast, two stubby, thumb-like sausages and slices of something dark and round and flat that Shadow didn't recognise.

'What's this?' asked Shadow.

'Black pudden,' said the man sitting next to him. He was one of the security guards, and was reading a copy of yesterday's *Sun* as he ate. 'Blood and herbs. They cook the blood until it congeals into a sort of a dark, herby scab.' He forked some eggs on to his toast, ate it with his fingers. 'I don't know. What is it they say, you should never see anyone making sausages or the law? Something like that.'

Shadow ate the rest of the breakfast, but he left the black pudding alone.

There was a pot of real coffee, now, and he drank a mug of it, hot and black, to wake him up and to clear his head.

Smith walked in. 'Shadow-man. Can I borrow you for five minutes?'

The Monarch of the Glen

'You're paying,' said Shadow. They walked out into the corridor.

'It's Mr Alice,' said Smith. 'He wants a quick word.' They crossed from the dismal whitewashed servants' wing into the wood-panelled vastness of the old house. They walked up the huge wooden staircase, and into a library. No one was there.

'He'll just be a minute,' said Smith. 'I'll make sure he knows you're waiting.'

The books in the library were protected from mice and dust and people by locked doors of glass and wire mesh. There was a painting of a stag on the wall, and Shadow walked over to look at it. The stag was haughty, and superior; behind it a valley filled with mist.

'*The Monarch of the Glen*,' said Mr Alice, walking in slowly, leaning on his stick. 'The most reproduced picture of Victorian times. That's not the original, but it was done by Landseer in the late 1850s as a copy of his own painting. I love it, although I'm sure I shouldn't. He did the lions in Trafalgar Square, Landseer. Same bloke.'

He walked over to the bay window, and Shadow walked with him. Below them, in the courtyard, servants were putting out chairs and tables. By the pond in the centre of the courtyard other people, party guests Shadow could see, were building bonfires out of logs and wood.

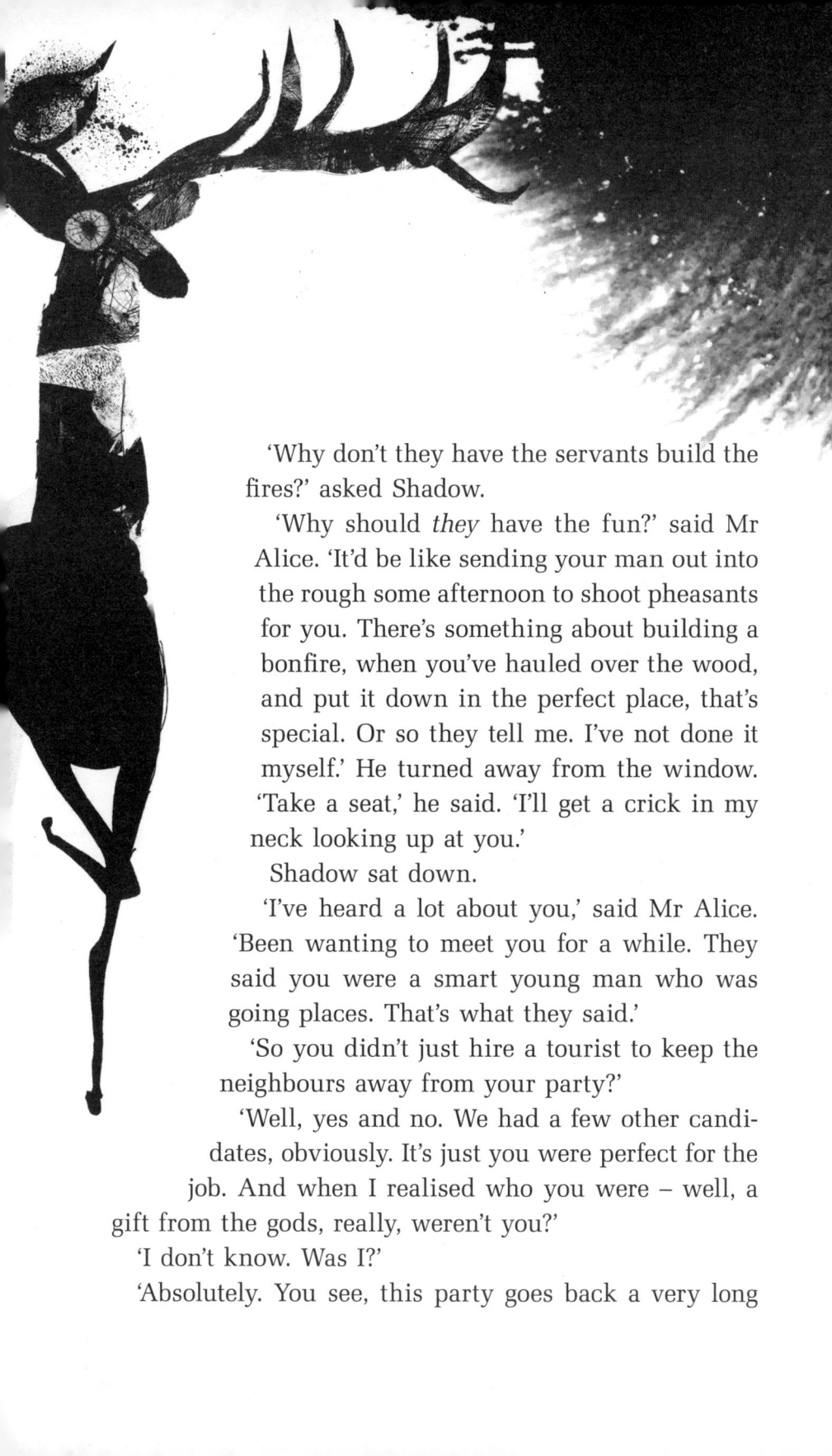

'Why don't they have the servants build the fires?' asked Shadow.

'Why should *they* have the fun?' said Mr Alice. 'It'd be like sending your man out into the rough some afternoon to shoot pheasants for you. There's something about building a bonfire, when you've hauled over the wood, and put it down in the perfect place, that's special. Or so they tell me. I've not done it myself.' He turned away from the window. 'Take a seat,' he said. 'I'll get a crick in my neck looking up at you.'

Shadow sat down.

'I've heard a lot about you,' said Mr Alice. 'Been wanting to meet you for a while. They said you were a smart young man who was going places. That's what they said.'

'So you didn't just hire a tourist to keep the neighbours away from your party?'

'Well, yes and no. We had a few other candidates, obviously. It's just you were perfect for the job. And when I realised who you were – well, a gift from the gods, really, weren't you?'

'I don't know. Was I?'

'Absolutely. You see, this party goes back a very long

way. Almost a thousand years, they've been having it. Never missed a single year. And every year there's a fight, between our man and their man. And our man wins. This year, our man is you.'

'Who . . .' said Shadow. 'Who are *they*? And who are *you*?'

'I am your host,' said Mr Alice. 'I suppose . . .' He stopped, for a moment, tapped his walking-stick against the wooden floor. '*They* are the ones who lost, a long time ago. *We* won. We were the knights, and they were the dragons, we were the giant-killers, they were the ogres. We were the men and they were the monsters. And *we won*. They know their place now. And tonight is all about not letting them forget it. It's humanity you'll be fighting for tonight. We can't let them get the upper hand. Not even a little. Us versus them.'

'Doctor Gaskell said that I was a monster,' said Shadow.

'Doctor Gaskell?' said Mr Alice. 'Friend of yours?'

'No,' said Shadow. 'He works for you. Or for the people who work for you. I think he kills children, and takes pictures of them.'

Mr Alice dropped his walking-stick. He bent down, awkwardly, to pick it up. Then he said, 'Well, I don't think you're a monster, Shadow. I think you're a hero.'

No, thought Shadow. *You think I'm a monster. But you think I'm* your *monster.*

'Now, you do well tonight,' said Mr Alice, 'and I know you will, and you can name your price. You ever wondered why some people were film stars, or famous, or rich? Bet you think, He's got no talent. What's he got that I haven't got? Well, sometimes the answer is, he's got someone like me on his side.'

'Are you a god?' asked Shadow.

Mr Alice laughed then, a deep, full-throated chuckle. 'Nice one, Mister Moon. Not at all. I'm just a boy from Streatham who's done well for himself.'

'So who do I fight?' asked Shadow.

'You'll meet him tonight,' said Mr Alice. 'Now, there's stuff needs to come down from the attic. Why don't you lend Smithie a hand? Big lad like you, it'll be a doddle.'

The audience was over and, as if on cue, Smith walked in.

'I was just saying,' said Mr Alice, 'that our boy here would help you bring the stuff down from the attic.'

'Triffic,' said Smith. 'Come on, Shadow. Let's wend our way upwards.'

They went up, through the house, up a dark wooden stairway, to a padlocked door, which Smith unlocked, into a dusty wooden attic, piled high with what looked like . . .

'Drums?' said Shadow.

'Drums,' said Smith. They were made of wood and of animal skins. Each drum was a different size. 'Right, let's take them down.'

They carried the drums downstairs. Smith carried one at a time, holding it as if it was precious. Shadow carried two.

'So what really happens tonight?' asked Shadow, on their third trip, or perhaps their fourth.

'Well,' said Smith, 'most of it, as I understand, you're best off figuring out on your own. As it happens.'

'And you and Mr Alice. What part do you play in this?'

Smith gave him a sharp look. They put the drums down at the foot of the stairs, in the great hall. There were several men there, talking in front of the fire.

When they were back up the stairs again, and out of earshot of the guests, Smith said, 'Mr Alice will be leaving us late this afternoon. I'll stick around.'

'He's leaving? Isn't he part of this?'

Smith looked offended. 'He's the host,' he said. 'But.' He stopped. Shadow understood. Smith didn't talk about his employer. They carried more drums down the stairs. When they had brought down all the drums, they carried down heavy leather bags.

'What's in these?' asked Shadow.

'Drumsticks,' said Smith.

Smith continued, 'They're old families. That lot downstairs. Very old money. They know who's boss, but that doesn't make him one of them. See? They're the only ones who'll be at tonight's party. They'd not want Mr Alice. See?'

And Shadow did see. He wished that Smith hadn't spoken to him about Mr Alice. He didn't think Smith would have said anything to anyone he thought would live to talk about it.

But all he said was, 'Heavy drumsticks.'

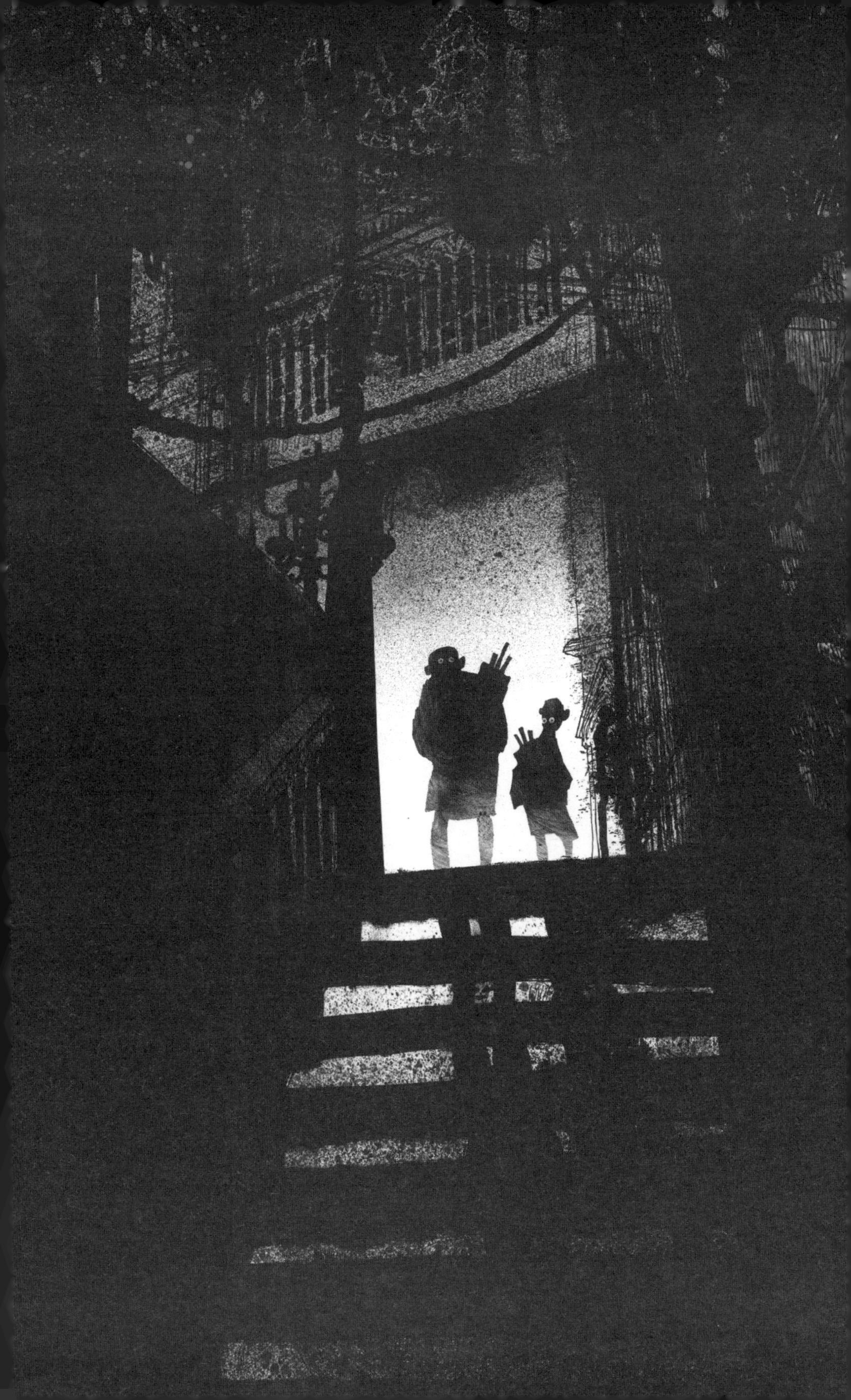

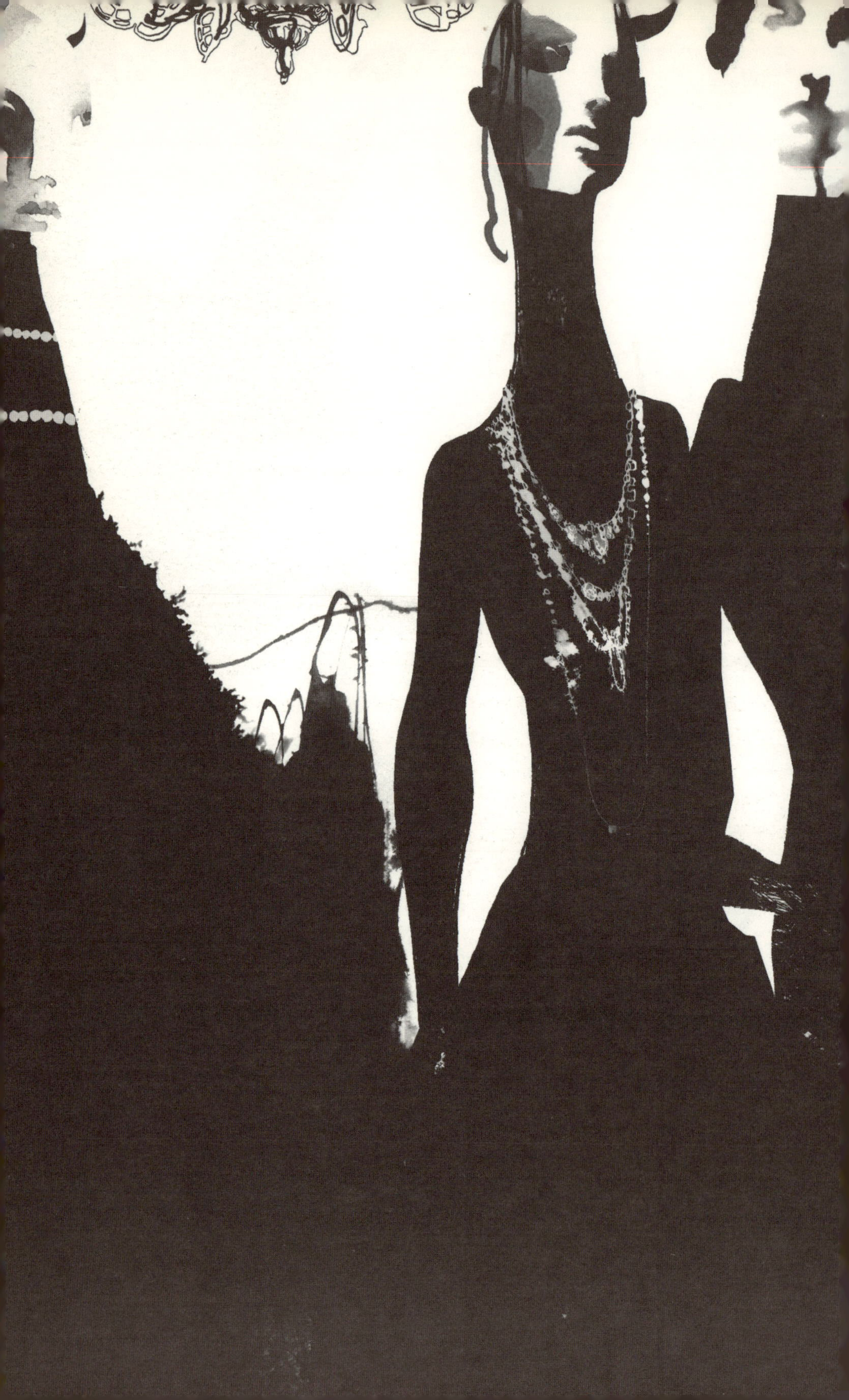

VIII

A small helicopter took Mr Alice away late that afternoon. Land-Rovers took away the staff. Smith drove the last one. Only Shadow was left behind, and the guests, with their smart clothes, and their smiles.

They stared at Shadow as if he were a captive lion who had been brought for their amusement, but they did not talk to him.

The dark-haired woman, the one who had smiled at Shadow as she had arrived, brought him food to eat: a steak, almost rare. She brought it to him on a plate, without cutlery, as if she expected him to eat it with his fingers and his teeth, and he was hungry, and he did.

'I am not your hero,' he told them, but they would not meet his gaze. Nobody spoke to him, not directly. He felt like an animal.

And then it was dusk. They led Shadow to the inner courtyard, by the rusty fountain, and they stripped him naked, at gunpoint, and the women smeared his body with some kind of thick yellow grease, rubbing it in.

They put a knife on the grass in front of him. A gesture with a gun, and Shadow picked the knife up. The hilt was black metal, rough and easy to hold. The blade looked sharp.

Then they threw open the great door, from the inner courtyard to the world outside, and two of the men lit the two high bonfires: they crackled and blazed.

They opened the leather bags, and each of the guests took out a single carved black stick, like a cudgel, knobbly and heavy. Shadow found himself thinking of Sawney Beane's children, swarming up from the darkness holding clubs made of human thigh-bones . . .

Then the guests arranged themselves around the edge of the courtyard and they began to beat the drums with the sticks.

They started slow, and they started quietly, a deep, throbbing pounding, like a heartbeat. Then they began to crash and slam into strange rhythms, staccato beats that wove and wound, louder and louder, until they filled Shadow's mind and his world. It seemed to him that the firelight flickered to the rhythms of the drums.

And then, from outside the house, the howling began.

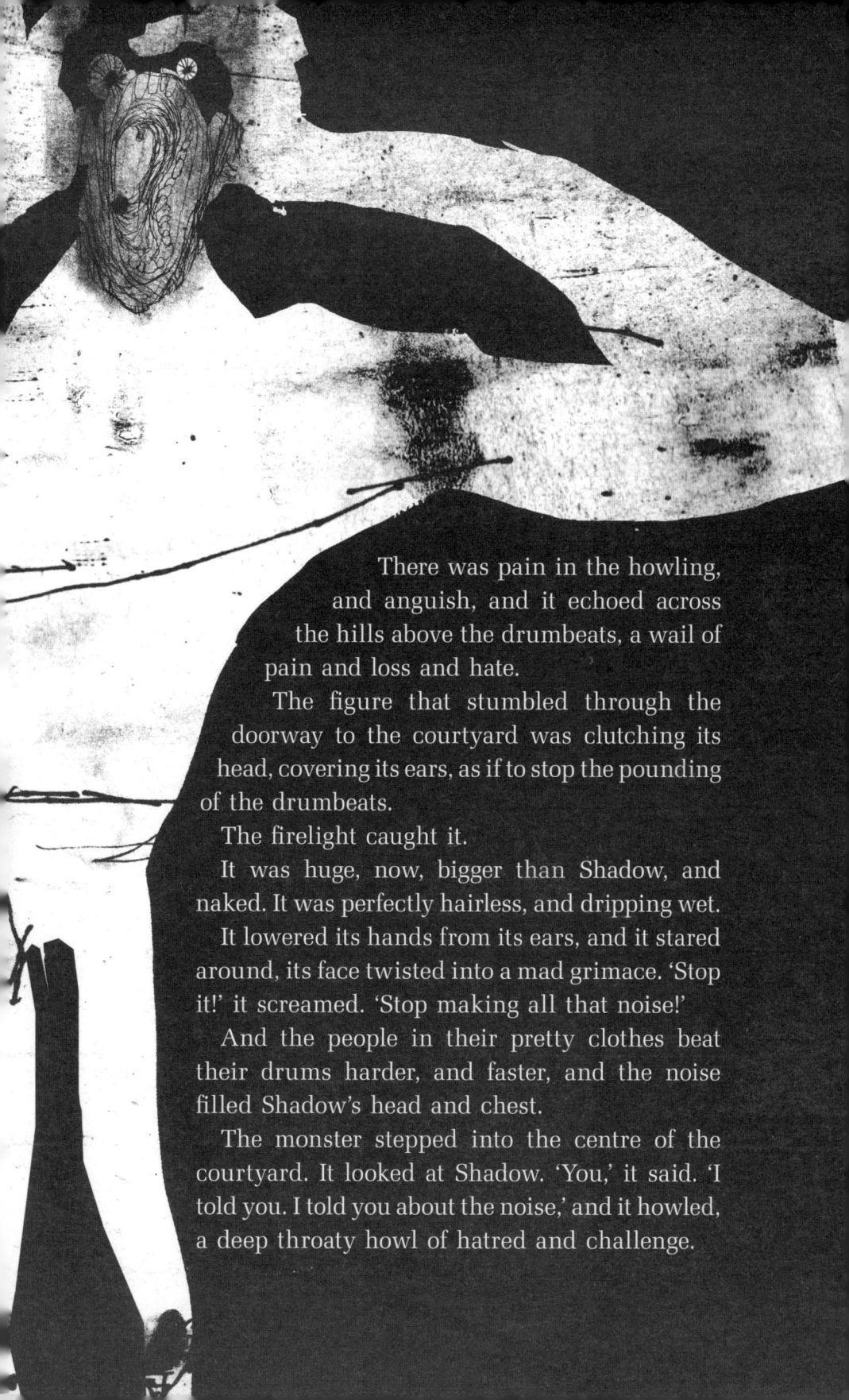

There was pain in the howling, and anguish, and it echoed across the hills above the drumbeats, a wail of pain and loss and hate.

The figure that stumbled through the doorway to the courtyard was clutching its head, covering its ears, as if to stop the pounding of the drumbeats.

The firelight caught it.

It was huge, now, bigger than Shadow, and naked. It was perfectly hairless, and dripping wet.

It lowered its hands from its ears, and it stared around, its face twisted into a mad grimace. 'Stop it!' it screamed. 'Stop making all that noise!'

And the people in their pretty clothes beat their drums harder, and faster, and the noise filled Shadow's head and chest.

The monster stepped into the centre of the courtyard. It looked at Shadow. 'You,' it said. 'I told you. I told you about the noise,' and it howled, a deep throaty howl of hatred and challenge.

The creature edged closer to Shadow. It saw the knife, and stopped. 'Fight me!' it shouted. 'Fight me fair! Not with cold iron! Fight me!'

'I don't want to fight you,' said Shadow. He dropped the knife on to the grass, raised his hands to show them empty.

'Too late,' said the bald thing that was not a man. 'Too late for that.'

And it launched itself at Shadow.

Later, when Shadow thought of that fight, he remembered only fragments: he remembered being slammed to the ground, and throwing himself out of the way. He remembered the pounding of the drums, and the expressions on the faces of the drummers as they stared, hungrily, between the bonfires, at the two men in the firelight.

They fought, wrestling and pounding each other.

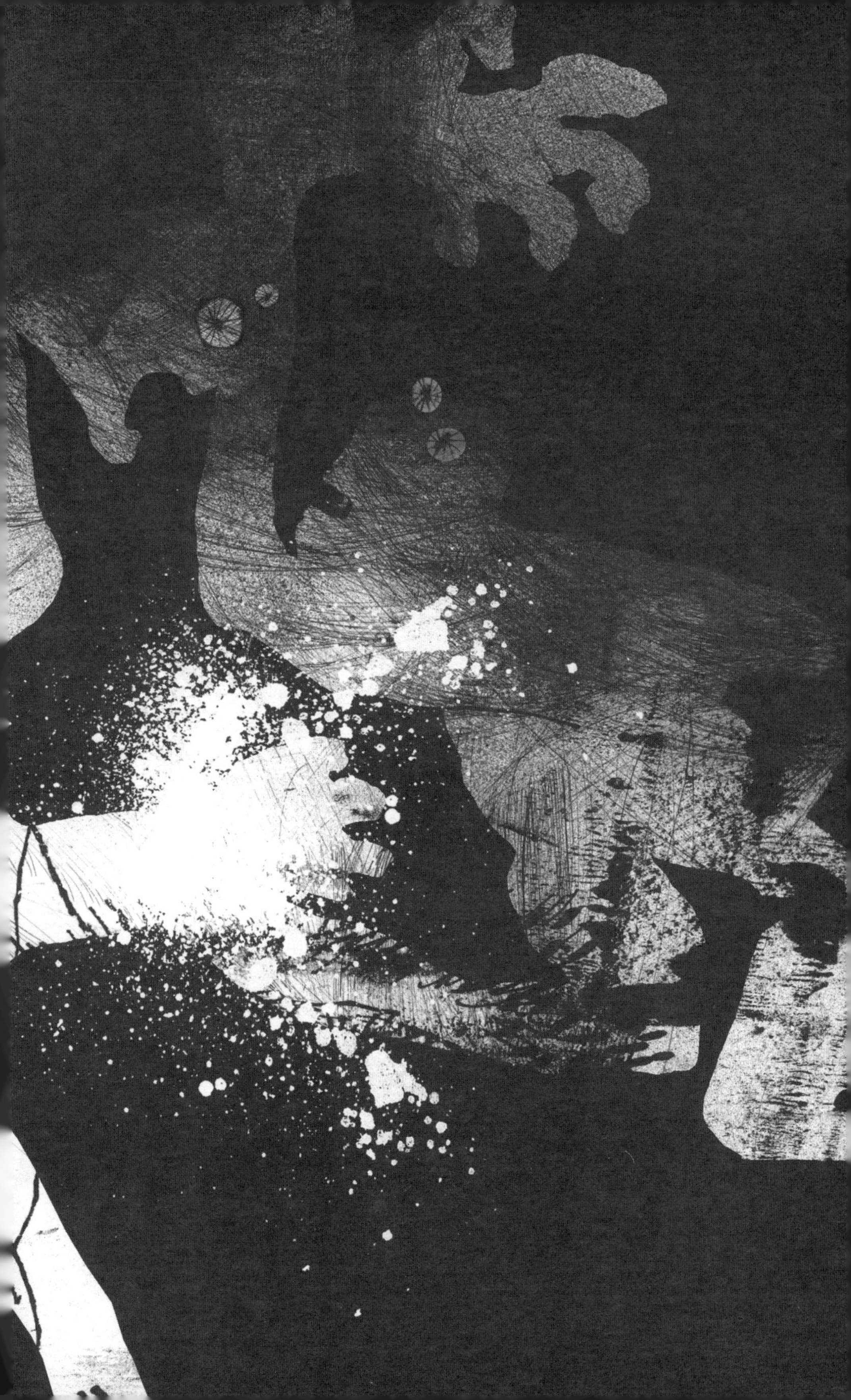

Salt tears ran down the monster's face as it wrestled with Shadow. They were equally matched, it seemed to Shadow.

The monster slammed its arm into Shadow's face, and Shadow tasted his own blood. He could feel his own anger beginning to rise, like a red wall of hate.

He swung a leg out, hooking the monster behind the knee, and as it stumbled back Shadow's fist crashed into its gut, making it cry out and roar with anger and pain.

A glance at the guests: Shadow saw the blood-lust on the faces of the drummers.

There was a cold wind, a sea-wind, and it seemed to Shadow that there were huge shadows in the sky, vast figures that he had seen on a ship made of the fingernails of dead men, and that they were staring down at him, that this fight was what was keeping them frozen on their ship, unable to land, unable to leave.

This fight was old, Shadow thought, older than even Mr Alice knew, and he was thinking that even as the creature's talons raked his chest. It was the fight of man against monster, and it was as old as time: it was Theseus battling the Minotaur, it was Beowulf and Grendel, it was every hero who had ever stood between the firelight and the darkness and wiped the blood of something inhuman from his sword.

The bonfires burned, and the drums pounded and throbbed and pulsed like the beating of a thousand hearts.

Shadow slipped on the damp grass, as the monster came at him, and he was down. The creature's fingers were around Shadow's neck, and it was squeezing; Shadow could feel everything starting to thin, to become distant.

He closed his hand around a patch of grass, and pulled at it, dug his fingers deep, grabbing a handful of grass and clammy earth, and he smashed the clod of dirt into the monster's face, momentarily blinding it.

He pushed up, and was on top of the creature, now. He rammed his knee hard into its groin, and it doubled into a foetal position, and howled, and sobbed.

Shadow realised that the drumming had stopped, and he looked up.

The guests had put down their drums.

They were all approaching him, in a circle, men and women, still holding their drumsticks, but holding them like cudgels. They were not looking at Shadow, though: they were staring at the monster on the ground, and they raised their black sticks and moved towards it in the light of the twin fires.

Shadow said, 'Stop!'

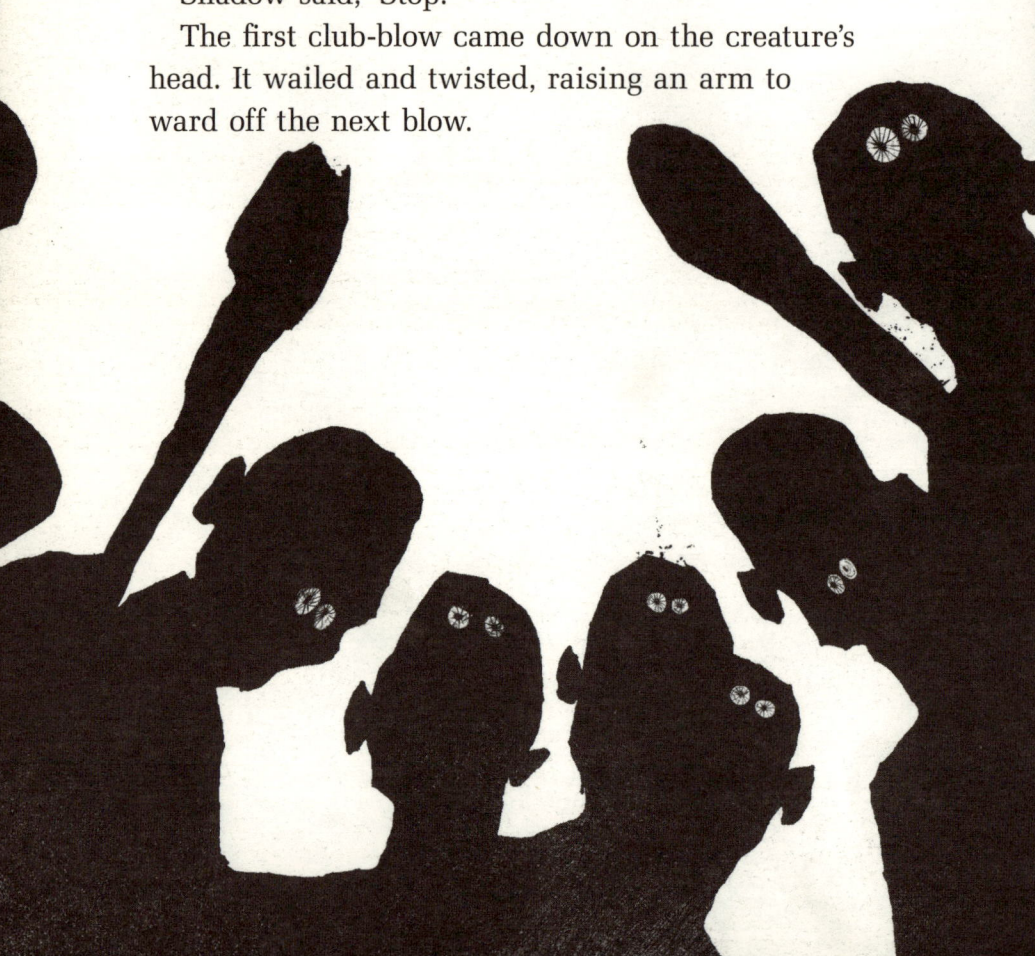

The first club-blow came down on the creature's head. It wailed and twisted, raising an arm to ward off the next blow.

Shadow threw himself in front of it, shielding it with his body. The dark-haired woman who had smiled at him before now brought down her club on his shoulder, dispassionately, and another club, from a man this time, hit him a numbing blow in the leg, and third struck him on his side.

They'll kill us both, he thought. *Him first, then me. That's what they do. That's what they always do.* And then, *She said she would come. If I called her.*

Shadow whispered, 'Jennie?'

There was no reply. Everything was happening so slowly. Another club was coming down, this one aimed at his hand. Shadow rolled out of the way awkwardly, watched the heavy wood smash into the turf.

'Jennie,' he said, picturing her too-fair hair in his mind, her thin face, her smile.

'I call you. Come now. *Please*.'

A gust of cold wind.

The dark-haired woman had raised her club high, and brought it down now, fast, hard, aiming for Shadow's face.

The blow never landed. A small hand caught the heavy stick as if it were a twig.

Fair hair blew about her head, in the cold wind. He could not have told you what she was wearing.

She looked at him. Shadow thought that she looked disappointed.

One of the men aimed a cudgel-blow at the back of her head. It never connected. She turned . . .

A rending sound, as if something was tearing itself apart . . .

And then the bonfires exploded. That was how it seemed. There was blazing wood all over the courtyard, even in the house. And the people were screaming in the bitter wind.

Shadow staggered to his feet.

The monster lay on the ground, bloodied and twisted. Shadow did not know if it was alive or not. He picked it up, hauled it over his shoulder, and staggered out of the courtyard with it.

He stumbled out on to the gravel forecourt, as the massive wooden doors slammed closed behind them. Nobody else would be coming out. Shadow kept moving down the slope, one step at a time, down towards the loch.

When he reached the water's edge he stopped, and sank to his knees, and let the bald man down on to the grass as gently as he could.

He heard something crash, and looked back up the hill.

The house was burning.

'How is he?' said a woman's voice.

Shadow turned. She was knee deep in the water, the creature's mother, wading towards the shore.

'I don't know,' said Shadow. 'He's hurt.'

'You're both hurt,' she said. 'You're all bluid and bruises.'

'Yes,' said Shadow.

'Still,' she said, 'he's not dead. And that makes a nice change.'

She had reached the shore now. She sat on the bank, with her son's head in her lap. She took a packet of tissues from her handbag, and spat on a tissue, and began fiercely to scrub at her son's face with it, rubbing away the blood.

The house on the hill was roaring now. Shadow had not imagined that a burning house would make so much noise.

The old woman looked up at the sky. She made a noise in the back of her throat, a

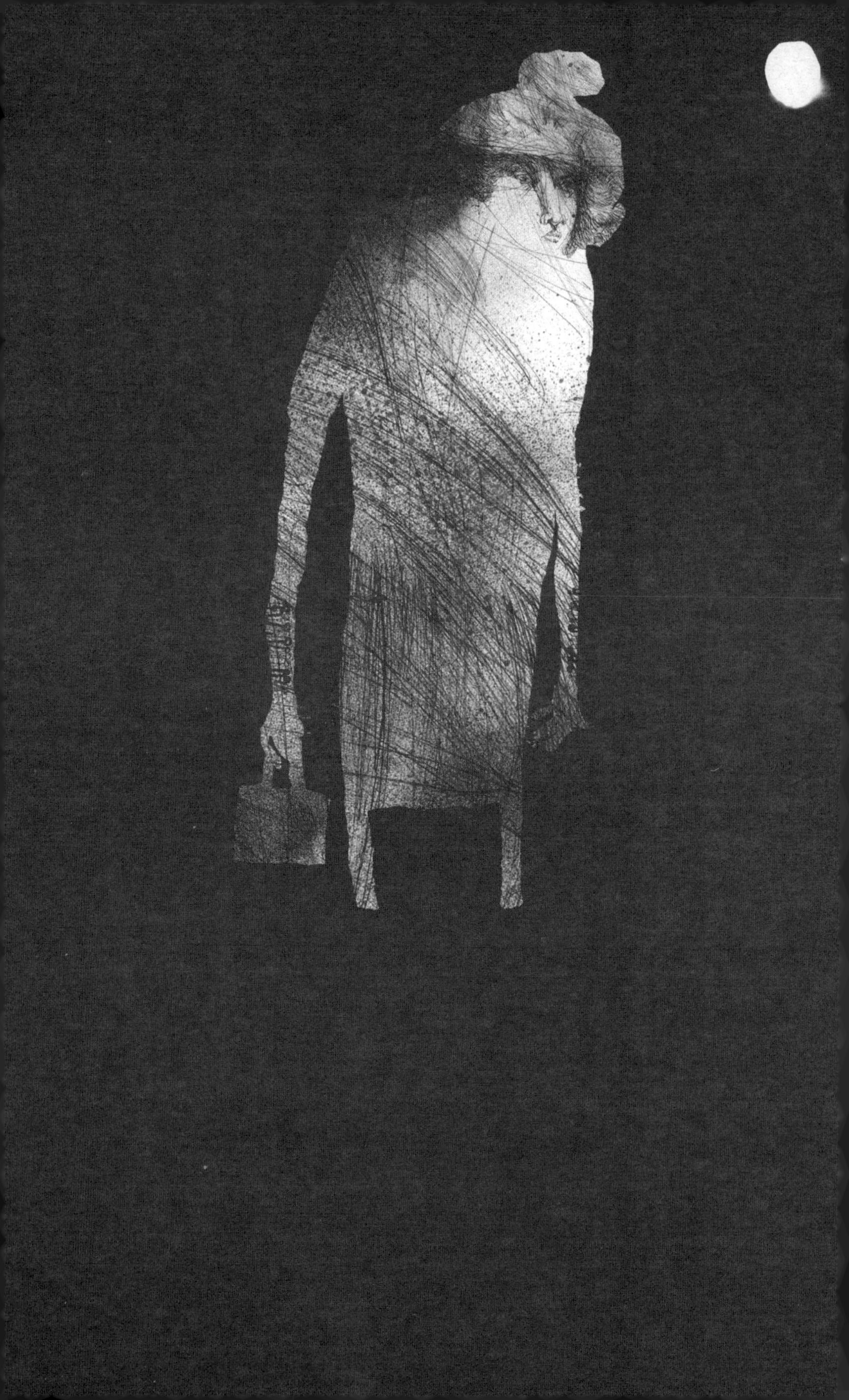

clucking noise, and then she shook her head. 'You know,' she said, 'you've let them in. They'd been bound for so long, and you've let them in.'

'Is that a good thing?' asked Shadow.

'I don't know, love,' said the little woman, and she shook her head again. She crooned to her son as if he were still her baby, and dabbed at his wounds with her spit.

Shadow was naked, at the edge of the loch, but the heat from the burning building kept him warm. He watched the reflected flames in the glassy water of the loch. A yellow moon was rising.

He was starting to hurt. Tomorrow, he knew, he would hurt much worse.

Footsteps on the grass behind him. He looked up. 'Hello, Smithie,' said Shadow.

Smith looked down at the three of them. 'Shadow,' he said, shaking his head. 'Shadow, Shadow, Shadow, Shadow, Shadow. This was not how things were meant to turn out.'

'Sorry,' said Shadow.

'This will cause real embarrassment to Mr Alice,' said Smith. 'Those people were his guests.'

'They were animals,' said Shadow.

'If they were,' said Smith, 'they were rich and important animals. There'll be widows and orphans and God knows what to take care of. Mr Alice will not be pleased.' He said it like a judge pronouncing a death sentence.

'Are you threatening him?' asked the old lady.

'I don't threaten,' said Smith, flatly.

She smiled. 'Ah,' she said. 'Well, I do. And if you or that fat bastard you work for hurt this young man, it'll be the worse for both of you.' She smiled then, with sharp teeth, and Shadow felt the hairs on the back of his neck prickle. 'There's worse things than dying,' she said. 'And I know most of them. I'm not young, and I'm not one for idle talk. So if I were you,' she said, with a sniff, 'I'd look after this lad.'

She picked up her son with one arm, as if he were a child's doll, and she clutched her handbag close to her with the other.

Then she nodded to Shadow, and walked away, into the glass-dark water, and soon she and her son were gone beneath the surface of the loch.

'Fuck,' muttered Smith.

Shadow didn't say anything.

Smith fumbled in his pocket. He pulled out the pouch of tobacco, and rolled himself a cigarette. Then he lit it. 'Right,' he said.

'Right?' said Shadow.

'We better get you cleaned up, and find you some clothes. You'll catch your death, otherwise. You heard what she said.'

Grendel

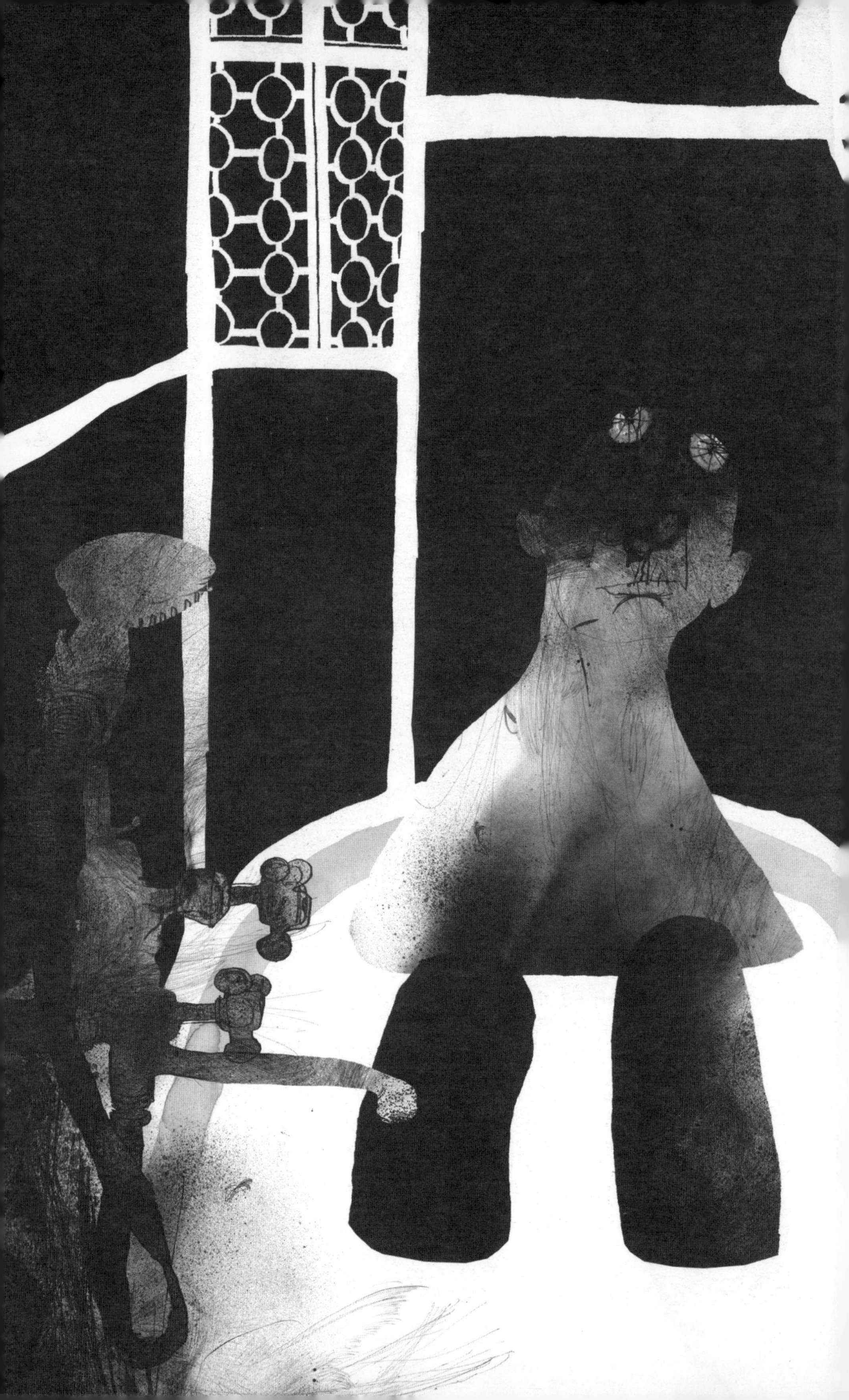

IX

They had the best room waiting for Shadow, that night, back at the hotel. And, less than an hour after Shadow returned, Gordon on the front desk brought up a new backpack for him, a box of new clothes, even new boots. He asked no questions.

There was a large envelope on top of the pile of clothes. Shadow ripped it open. It contained his passport, slightly scorched, his wallet, and money: several bundles of new fifty-pound notes, wrapped in rubber bands. *My God, how the money rolls in*, he thought, without pleasure, and tried, without success, to remember where he had heard that song before.

He took a long bath, to soak away the pain.

And then he slept.

In the morning he dressed, and walked up the lane next to the hotel that led up the hill and out of the village. There had been a cottage at the top of the hill, he was sure of it, with lavender in the garden, a stripped pine counter-top and a purple sofa, but no matter where he looked there was no cottage on the hill, nor any evidence that there ever had been anything there but grass and a hawthorn tree.

He called her name, but there was no reply, only the wind coming in off the sea, bringing with it the first promises of winter.

Still, she was waiting for him, when he got back to the hotel room. She was sitting on the bed, wearing her old brown coat, inspecting her fingernails. She did not look up when he unlocked the door and walked in.

'Hello, Jennie,' he said.

'Hello,' she said. Her voice was very quiet.

'Thank you,' he said. 'You saved my life.'

'You called,' she said dully. 'I came.'

He said, 'What's wrong?'

She looked at him, then. 'I could have been yours,' she said, and there were tears in her eyes. 'I thought you would love me. Perhaps. One day.'

'Well,' he said, 'maybe we could find out. We could take a walk tomorrow together, maybe. Not a long one, I'm afraid, I'm a bit of a mess physically.'

She shook her head.

The strangest thing, Shadow thought, was that she did not look human any longer: she now looked like what she was, a wild thing, a forest thing. Her tail twitched on the bed, under her coat. She was very beautiful, and, he realised, he wanted her, very badly.

'The hardest thing about being a *hulder*,' said Jennie, 'even a *hulder* very far from home, is that, if you don't want to be lonely, you have to love a man.'

'So love me. Stay with me,' said Shadow. 'Please.'

'You,' she said, sadly and finally, 'are not a man.'

She stood up.

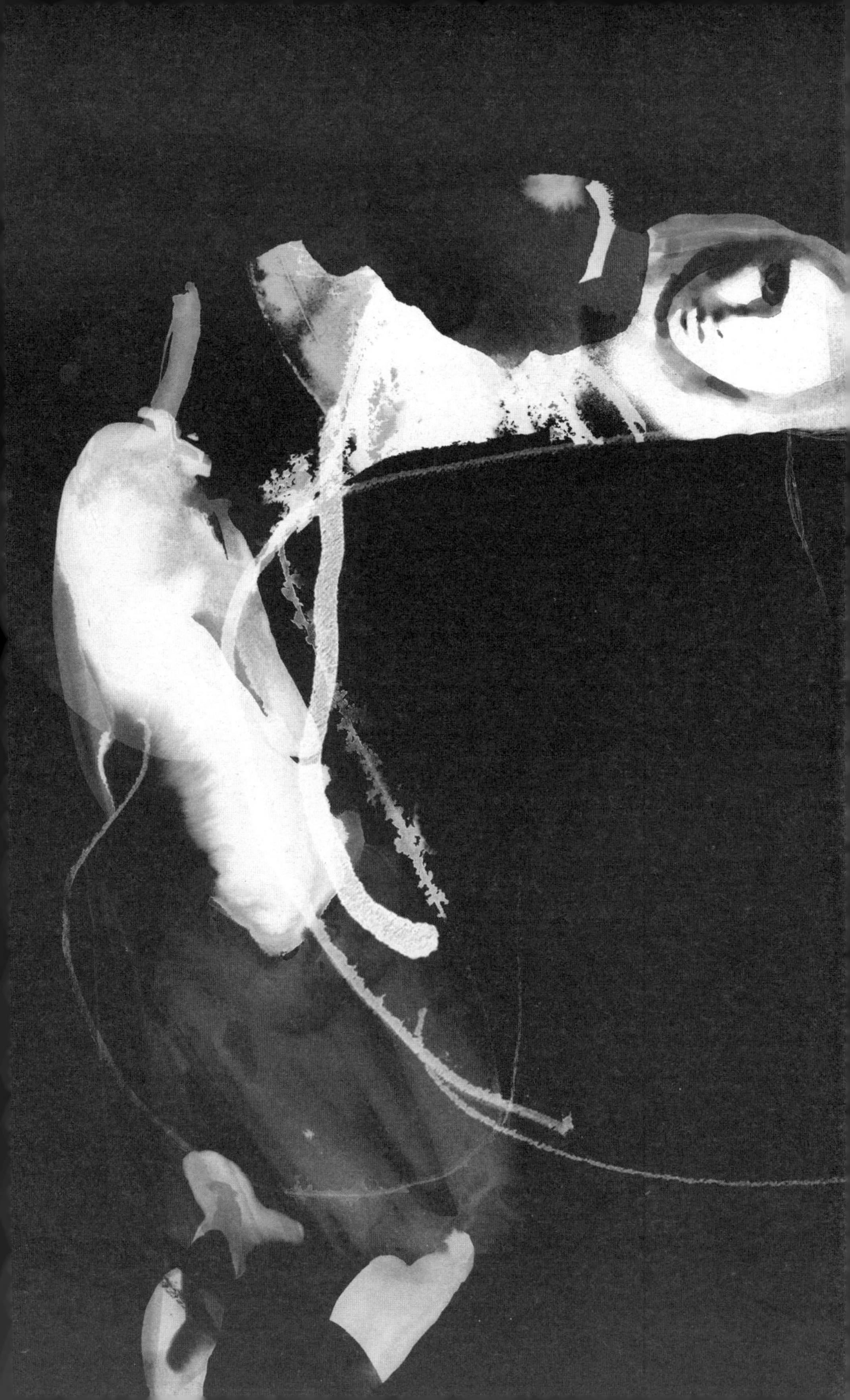

'Still,' she said, 'everything's changing. Maybe I can go home again now. After a thousand years I don't even know if I remember any *norsk*.'

She took his hands in her small hands, which could bend iron bars, which could crush rocks to sand, and she squeezed his fingers very gently. And she was gone.

He stayed another day in that hotel, and then he caught the bus to Thurso, and the train from Thurso to Inverness.

He dozed on the train, although he did not dream.

When he woke, there was a man on the seat next to him. A hatchet-faced man, reading a paperback book. He closed the book when he saw that Shadow was awake. Shadow looked down at the cover: Jean Cocteau's *The Difficulty of Being*. 'Good book?' asked Shadow.

'Yeah, all right,' said Smith. 'It's all essays. They're meant to be personal, but you feel that every time he looks up innocently and says, "This is me," it's some kind of double-bluff. I liked *Belle et la Bête*, though. I felt closer to him watching that than through any of these essays.'

'It's all on the cover,' said Shadow.

'How d'you mean?'

'The difficulty of being Jean Cocteau.'

Smith scratched his nose.

'Here,' he said. He passed Shadow a copy of the *Scotsman*. 'Page nine.'

At the bottom of page nine was a small story: retired doctor kills himself. Gaskell's body had been found in his car, parked in a picnic spot on the coast road. He had swallowed quite a cocktail of painkillers, washed down with most of a bottle of Lagavulin.

'Mr Alice hates being lied to,' said Smith. 'Especially by the hired help.'

'Is there anything in there about the fire?' asked Shadow.

'What fire?'

'Oh. Right.'

'It wouldn't surprise me if there wasn't a terrible run of luck for the great and the good over the next couple of months, though. Car crashes. Train crash. Maybe a plane'll go down. Grieving widows and orphans and boyfriends. Very sad.'

Shadow nodded.

'You know,' said Smith, 'Mr Alice is very concerned about your health. He worries. I worry too.'

'Yeah?' said Shadow.

'Absolutely. I mean, if something happens to you while you're in the country. Maybe you look the wrong way crossing the road. Flash a wad of cash in the wrong pub. I dunno. The point is, if you got hurt, then whatsername, Grendel's mum, might take it the wrong way.'

'So?'

'So we think you should leave the UK. Be safer for everyone, wouldn't it?'

Shadow said nothing for a while. The train began to slow.

'Okay,' said Shadow.

'This is my stop,' said Smith. 'I'm getting out here. We'll arrange the ticket, first class, of course, to anywhere you're heading. One-way ticket. You just have to tell me where you want to go.'

Shadow rubbed the bruise on his cheek. There was something about the pain that was almost comforting.

The train came to a complete stop. It was a small station, seemingly in the middle of nowhere. There was a large black car parked by the building, in the thin sunshine.

The windows were tinted, and Shadow could not see inside.

Smith pushed down the train window, reached outside to open the carriage door, and he stepped out on to the platform. He looked back in at Shadow through the open window. 'Well?'

'I think,' said Shadow, 'that I'll spend a couple of weeks looking around the UK. And you'll just have to pray that I look the right way when I cross your roads.'

'And then?'

Shadow knew it, then. Perhaps he had known it all along.

'Chicago,' he said to Smith, as the train gave a jerk, and began to move away from the station. He felt older, as he said it. But he could not put it off for ever.

And then he said, so quietly that only he could have heard it, 'I guess I'm going home.'

Soon afterwards it began to rain: huge, pelting drops that rattled against the windows and blurred the world into greys and greens. Deep rumbles of thunder accompanied Shadow on his journey south: the storm grumbled, the wind howled and the lightning made huge shadows across the sky, and in their company Shadow slowly began to feel less alone.

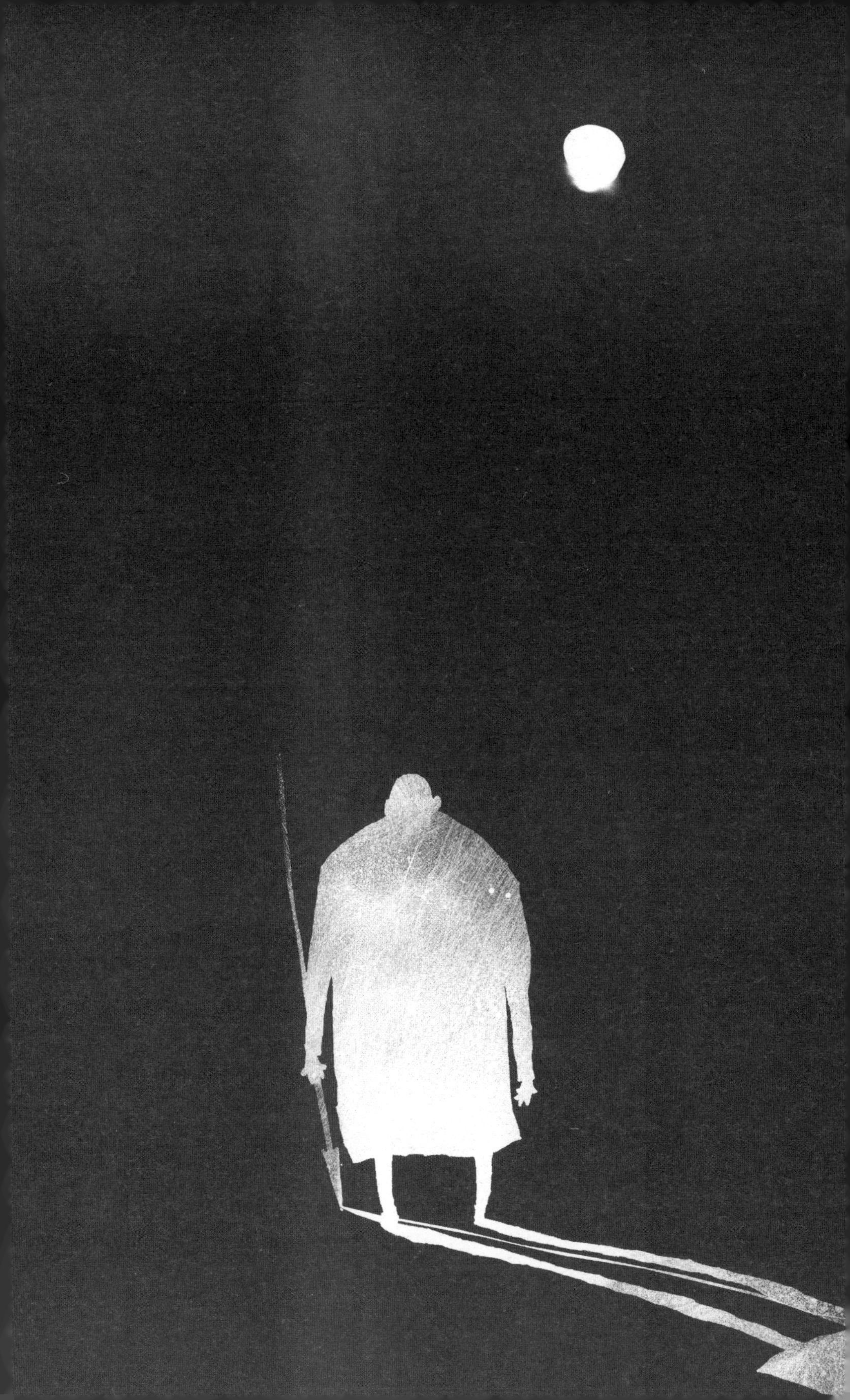

NEIL GAIMAN
AMERICAN GODS

Would you believe that all the gods that people have ever imagined are still with us today?

Available now from

HEADLINE

NEIL GAIMAN
ANANSI BOYS

Anansi was a spider, when the world was young, and all the stories were being told for the first time. He used to get himself into trouble, and he used to get himself out of trouble. The story of the tar-baby, the one they tell about Brer Rabbit? That was Anansi's story first. Some people think he was a rabbit. But that's their mistake. He wasn't a rabbit. He was a spider.

Available now from

HEADLINE

NEIL GAIMAN
BLACK DOG

The locals say that on a clear night, which tonight certainly is not, you can find yourself being followed by Black Shuck. He's a sort of a fairy dog. If you see him – you die.

Available now from

HEADLINE